I0612893

LIFE SONGS

A Selection of Poems

BY JACK RANDOM

CROW DOG PRESS
TURLOCK CA USA

Life Songs

A Selection of Poems

By Jack Random

Published by
Crow Dog Press
1241 Windsor Court
Turlock CA 95380

Cover art by Ray Miller.

ISBN-13: 978-0-9977883-7-2

LIFE SONGS

A Selection of Poems

JACK FOLEY ON LIFE SONGS

Ray Miller (Jack Random) writes, "Poetry has long been like a secret love for which I never had enough time." The "time" of these poems – these "life songs" – is the time of all poetry: the now, the moment, the sudden onset of awareness:

Faces drawn by worried hands
Fingers clench as if in prayer
Eyes seeking understanding
Silence stills the air

Formally, these poems tend to be ballads, song lyrics even: they often rhyme, they are (the big A in poetry!) Accessible. They can usually be taken in at a single reading. You are not likely to find references to Chaucer, Rumi, Mallarmé or Richard Wagner in their cadences, though Charles Bukowski and Tom Waits and even Baudelaire do make appearances. They are fundamentally in the great tradition of Kipling's "Barrack Room Ballads" or even Robert W. Service's memorable story-telling poems. This is not to say that Random's poems lack depth – depth they have aplenty: only to say that they lack the desire to baffle the reader. They resemble popular songs in the sense that they insist on immediacy of impact: we are somewhere different when we finish them than we were when we began – and we are the better for it. Wonder is at their heart. Random writes magically of the cathedral of Notre Dame,

To have walked those hallowed grounds

In the cradle of western civilization
At the living heart of a continent...
To see it now in flames...
We are all Parisians now

Pay some attention to a poet who does not "foreground language," does not carry the weight of a doomed Western civilization on his shoulders, but who looks at the world with open eyes and an open – even an innocent – heart. You won't regret it.

Jack Foley
Oakland CA
June 2021

AUTHOR INTRODUCTION

I have devoted much of my adult life to writing. At various stages of my life I have devoted myself to plays, short stories, novels, political essays, and poetry. It seems I have saved the latter for the latter years of my life. It was not an intentional choice. It was simply how my life unfolded.

I began the daily ritual of writing poetry toward the end of 2019. As of this writing I have written close to nine hundred poems and I have divided them into three categories: *Poems for a Pandemic: The Coronavirus Series, Poemics: Poems of Social and Political Justice* and the selection you now endeavor to read: *Life Songs: A Selection of Poems.*

In many ways *Life Songs* is the work I set out to write when this adventure began. They are personal poems. They reflect not only the events of my life but – perhaps most importantly – how I look at and navigate the world. They represent my outlook, my philosophy and my values as an artist, a writer, and a human being.

Most of my creative work was undertaken with the idea that I could improve life on the planet. This selection is different. Although some may aspire to change in the hearts of my readers, these poems generally reflect my feelings and perceptions of the world around me.

While I have often been critical of my fellow human beings, these poems reflect a great affection and empathy for others within and without my life. For though I despise cruelty and injustice I have always believed that humans are in their essence good and kind. It is only when the indignities of life alter the fundamentals of the self that humans tend to do heartless things. Remove the hurt that bad actors carry within and they will emerge as kinder, better human beings.

These poems also reflect a great love of nature and the creative endeavors of my fellow artists. Poetry has long been like a secret love for which I never had enough time. Now, in what may be the twilight of my life, I have found the time.

I hope that you will enjoy these poems and find in them some morsel of inspiration and beauty.

Ray Miller (aka Jack Random)
Turlock CA
March 2021

TABLE OF CONTENTS

Life Songs

At the Table

Faces drawn by worried hands
Fingers clench as if in prayer
Eyes seeking understanding
Silence stills the air
Voices thin to hollow whisper
At the table of despair

We are gathered here
To share our sorrow
To mourn a passing soul
Remembering a heart so fair
So giving and so warm
At the table of despair

Reaching back for good times
In the comfort of our home
A smile cracks the darkness
Gentle laughter if we dare
She gives us all her blessings
At the table of despair

She is gone forever
Though her spirit here remains
To guide us through the sorrow
To mend the hearts that tear
We sigh and breathe again
At the table of despair

We raise a glass in tribute
As our stories make the round
Resurrect the joy she gave us

Though she is now an empty chair
We will say goodbye at least for now
To this table of despair

The Graceful Stumble

Black leather boots on fishnet stockings
Short tight skirt red silk blouse
Wild blonde hair frames mascara eyes
She owns the place from floor to ceiling

Scanning the room she settles on me
O happy day O blessed hour
Heart song of pounding ecstasy
She parts a sea of lesser beings
And presses her phone into my hand
I trace her glance to the one beside her
Hidden by my foolish passion

Take our picture, sport?

O horror O cursed reckoning
She sees the truth and freezes

My pleasure

I smile and square their joy in her device

Plains of Existence

A world upon a world upon a world upon a world
And I am but a wanderer searching for my own

A town upon a city upon a village upon a square
And I am but a visitor a long way from my home

Stars upon the heavens
Galaxies among the stars
And I am but a dreamer
Seeking answers where none are

All my life I've tread on slivers of thin ice
Always knowing this existence
Could scatter into a billion little pieces
Still I wander still I roam ever farther from my home
Ever seeking to know that which cannot be known

A world upon a world upon a world upon a world
And I am but a shadow in the prison of a tome

In the end as in the beginning we walk alone
We leave our loved ones behind
And pray to find fulfillment of our destinies
In this world or the next or the next or the next

A world upon a world upon a world upon a world
And I am but a stranger still searching for my own

Requiem for a Fighting Man

He was a fighting man
Born to a generation of war
Bruised and battered
Cornered and against the ropes
He never surrendered
Never gave in

He saw injustice and fought back
He saw brutality and stopped it
He saw bigotry and stood against it

He felt the crushing blows of retribution
The bitter sting of betrayal
He stumbled and faltered
But he never gave in

His god was knowledge
His religion truth
His gospel common sense

He was flawed like all men
He loved the ladies
He lived a second childhood
His mind lost its clarity
But he always held on to his pride
Even to the end

Notre Dame

The dream that shaped the vision
The hands that carved the stone
The devotion to intricate detail
The dedication to endure

To have walked those hallowed grounds
In the cradle of western civilization
At the living heart of a continent

She stands the millennia in tribute
To the best of the human spirit
To the city of dreamers and visionaries
To the soul of all artists
And the embrace of all lovers

To have entered that sacred citadel
To sit where Hugo might have sat
And dreamed of gypsy dancers
And lonely poets and love immortal

To have touched those ancient stones
And felt their truths coursing through my veins
To hear the bells that Quasimodo rang
And the songs the gypsies sang

To see it now in flames...
It crushes the soul and feeds a spiteful rage

The people of Paris gather to share their grief
To mourn to cry and sing
And I five thousand miles away

Stand in solidarity to feel their passion
And their pain

We are all Parisians now
Bonded in tears and love and faith

The cathedral will rise again
And all humanity will sing her praise

Slow and Easy (for Tom Waits)

Woke up on a fine summer day
Let the sun roll over my eyes
Decided I had nothing to do
But take the long way through the park
To the corner store on 2nd and Vine

Squirrels scampering dogs in flight
Mothers hustling with their kids in tow
Sat on a bench to have an old school toke
Watched a child six or seven
Trying to climb a tree

He'd rear back like a raging bull
Charge it like an enemy
On the battlefield of life

Tried two or three times four
But the tree spat him back like chewed gum
Till the child sat down near to tears

I strolled over and took the tree
In three long strides
Sat on a branch for a whistle
Fore I came back down again

One thing I learned about this life, kid
Take it slow and easy
Or don't take it at all

I tipped my hat and went my way

Pull the Thread

Follow the money
Pull the thread
You get too close
You end up dead

Growing up on the westside
You live by a code
Depends on who's asking
What you do or don't know

Brother gets shot on enemy ground
What he doing there
We be asking around
Cops say they don't know
But everybody know better
It's all wrote down
In the neighborhood letter

Follow the money
Pull the thread
You get too close
You gonna end up dead

Guns be pointing in every direction
But something don't fit
Like a glove that's all wrong
The cops be singing the same old song

Follow the money
Pull the thread
You get too close

Gonna end up dead

Cops be saying how it all went down
But the truth be buried six feet underground

Follow the money
Pull the thread
If you get too close
You gonna end up dead

Christmas in Manhattan

Am I dreaming or is this New York?
What possesses a man to wear a Christmas tree
Like it was an overcoat
Like he had nothing better to do than
Strap on a Christmas tree
And take a ride on the subway?

And if you did wear a Christmas tree
To take a ride on the subway
Would you really pull out your cellphone
To check your emails?

The strangest part is: no one notices
They're all too busy checking their own emails
And whatever else they do on their cellphones

Am I dreaming or is this New York?
One more Christmas in Manhattan
And I might as well check myself into
The nearest loony bin

I've got to get off this train
As if it's going to be any different on the street
It's a ride on the crazy train
In a town where crazy is cool
And everyone thrives on it

Fifth Avenue and 32nd Street
This is where I get off

God I love this town

Solstice in the Sierras

The scent of fresh clean pine
Sends me back to the Sierras
Where the winter carries a bite
And the sky is so clear
You can touch the stars

Comfort around a fire circle
Beneath a blanket with my love
The smell of hot cocoa
The crackle of sparks tracing upward
The smell of burning pine

The rising moon takes hold of the sky
Full and round like dreams of flight
Flickering light on smooth waters
A slow walk around the mill pond
Animal eyes pierce the darkness

Snowflakes flutter from the heavens
Planting kisses on our faces
The longest night the shortest day
As we embrace the hour

Solstice in the Sierras

Midwinter Deep

Awakening on a bed of snow
Scattered thoughts lost control
Senses drain from fingertips
Freezing to the depths of bone

Abandoned in this forsaken place
To discover the reasons why
To crack the skin of pretense
And carve away the lies

There is a coldness of the soul
Far greater than the bruising wind
Deeper than the deep unknown
More cutting than any sin

I live to taste my last cold breath
And touch the chilling night
And cast away my vagaries
And grasp the end of light

Did I place myself upon this ledge
Or was I tossed like something old
For there is everlasting peace they say
In yielding to the cold

Let it go let it be let it flow
Listen to the fluttering angels
Hear them calling through the pine
So seductive enchanting so divine

Awaken to the thump of heartbeat

Is it yours or is it mine
The wiz and whirl of medicine machines
A voice says you'll be fine

The biting cold receding now
The truth of what I've seen
Falling like a curtain
In the misty shadows of a dream

The Collection

Coins stamps baseball cards
Cars jewelry trophies art
The nature of the beast
The way of the Tao
The price of being human

We desire we possess
Until the things we possess
Possess us

For me it was postcards
Not tourist postcards
No landscapes or pastoral scenes
No Eschers or Picassos or Hoppers
No Yosemite landscapes

I collected heroes
The people I admire
Einstein Bogie James Dean
Geronimo Sitting Bull Black Elk
Mark Twain Poe & Shaw
Lennon Jimi & Janis
Kerouac Ginsberg Moriarty
DiMaggio Mantle Mays
Bacall Liz & Ingrid Bergman
Sweet Marilyn Monroe

Heroes heroes one and all
In the corners and on the walls
Bukowski Pollard Baudelaire
In my drawers and on my chairs

Crazy Horse and Bobby D
The more you have the more you need
Morrison Huxley Albert Gore
Comes a time to say no more

My life is my own after all
They had theirs and I have mine
To rise or fall or flounder
Like a drunken fish

I am myself
My hero and my villain
My all or nothing at all
For what it's worth
I am what I am alone

Nobody Knows I'm Here

Two hours on the casino floor
And my mind is rattling like a box of stones
I tell my wife I need a break
Walk back to the room
And there it is

A plain white envelope
Sitting on the bed
As if waiting for me
My name and room number
Scribbled in red ink
Casino logo where the return address
Should be no stamp
But nobody knows I'm here
Nobody but my wife

Must be the casino I surmise
I open the envelope
Two crisp one-hundred-dollar bills
Wrapped in a clean white
Sheet of paper I smile

Must be the casino
I call the front desk and inquire
No answers but simple advice
Enjoy your stay Mister Mills

Why not gamble it away
Free money and this is the place
I go down to the roulette table
Drop it all on red clickety clack
It comes up black

Go back to the room
And there it is by all appearances
The same envelope but not
In the place I left it

Sealed I open it
Two hundred bucks in plain white paper
I call my wife to ask what's what
Nobody knows I'm here
She laughs and wonders what
The problem is
Free money at a place to gamble

I go downstairs and fritter it away
Rush back to the room
And there it is
Two hundred bucks in clean white paper

I turn on the TV to ponder my options
An old show in black and gray
About a man who receives a gift
An unlimited cash supply
In the end it drives him crazy

I call the desk
I call the TV station
I call my wife
I call the police

Everyone has the same answer
You're a lucky man Mister Mills
Free money gamble it away

I try I do but I know the story
In the end it drives me crazy

Love is a Blanket

Love is a blanket
Embracing you on the coldest night
Love is a smile
Carrying you the last lonely mile

Some find solace in natural wonders
Some find purpose in the words of masters
Some wander the earth in search of meaning
I found it all in the warmth of her touch

Love is a blanket embracing your soul
Love is a smile that guides you home
Love is feeling without even knowing
Love is the giving without hesitation

I found love when I wasn't looking
Love found me when I came back home

Love waits
Love gives
Love bends
Love is

The Long Goodnight

In the long good night cicada sing
Wild dogs rumble through tall grass
Hunters sweep the forest floor
Creepers scramble for cover

In the long good night
Calm turns to terror
Joy turns to fear
Humans become beasts

Darkness spins a web of shadows
Casting virtue out of sight
Chasing dreams to waking tremor
Waiting for the light

In the long good night
Ill intent crawls out of cracks
Sheltered souls and evil deeds
Emerge from hidden places

In the long good night
We sleep we dream we cower
For life belongs to daylight
Death awaits the midnight hour

Romantic Love

The taste of your lips
The shape of your dance
The lilt of your smile
The grace of your gaze
At twilight

To have lived beneath your shelter
To have shared your dreams
To have bathed in the waves
Of your passion
To have breathed the air
That nurtures you
Fulfills and delights my soul

None should possess your beauty
Lest all the world collapse in envy

None should approach your perfection
Lest muses shrink and graces
Cower in shame

You are love sweet love
And I exist to sing your praise

Classic Blue

A blue so deep and true
It rises from the bowels of the earth
Azure

A tone so pure and pulsating
It awakens the depths of soul
Holiday blue

A skyline whispering twilight
Beneath a floating moon
Mystic blue

Waves of lingering sorrow
Tears of eternal longing
Mourning blue

Stars of distant galaxies
In fields of darkest light
Classic blue

The Wolf & the Creator

(after a drawing by Kananginak Pootoogook)

The creator makes the wolf
To rid the world of the weak
The old and infirm

Does the creator know
When she is old and feeble
The wolf will rid the world
Of her?

Does the wolf know
When he kills the creator
He kills himself?

The Game of Opposites

Lips rough as sandpaper
Grace of a bumbling bovine
The irony of your smirk
And the screech of your voice at midnight

To have breathed your morning stench
To have slept on your stained couch
To have bathed in your daily squalor
Is more than one soul can bear

No one should be so repulsive
Except to bring relief to the deformed
No one should smell so putrid
Except to repel rabid dogs

You are a horror among horrors
And I was born to revile your
Very existence

Connection Awareness Light

I am one with all
Despite my doubt

I love all beings
Despite self-loathing

I believe in goodness
Despite the horror

There is no evil
In the deepest heart of man

There is no hatred
In the greater soul of woman

There is no greed
There is no jealousy
When needs are fulfilled
And dreams are realized

We have only barriers to overcome
And common bonds to embrace

We live to seek wisdom
Not to do harm

We are one with all
And all is one within

Smile

(for Charlie Chaplin)

Ink drop on clean paper
Spreads and swallows all
That it touches

Shake it off let it go
Put on a smiley face

Starts in the gut
Wraps around my body
Swallows my will

Shake it off let it go
Pack it away

Paint the world in shadow
Slipping down the hole
Taking hold

Shake it off let it go
Take the day

What good is it to pretend
All is well when every breath
You take suffocates?

Shake it off let it go
Tomorrow is another day

Writing in the Dark

Legend has it Paine wrote
The times that try men's souls
On the head of a drum
In the New Jersey wilderness

Words that lit the flame of liberty
Defeated an army of empire
Words that carved the arch of history
And lifted the fate of humankind

One wonders what might have been
Had Einstein not a pen
And $E = MC$ squared slipped back
Into unconscious folds of memory

A pen! A pen! My kingdom for a pen!
I have lost more words than I could gain
From the libraries of ancient scribes
A word for every drop of rain

While Shakespeare wrote his folios
I have squandered volumes
Chasing pens and clearing time
Forging bonds of rhythmic meaning
Casting thoughts in rhyme

To immortalize our work our art
We all want to make our mark
But without space time and inspiration
We're writing in the dark

The Peace of Wild Things

The wild thrives on balance
Prey and predator
Growth and decay
Life and death
In eternal motion

There is no loyalty in nature
There is no greed or hatred
Hunters protect their territories
To survive not to conquer

In the wild there is no plotting
There is no fretting a cruel fate
All creatures live by instinct
Freedom is a constant state

No thoughts beyond the moment
No fear beyond the senses
To live to breathe to be
In that there is a calmness
A silence of the heart
In that there is a certain peace
And a place for us to start

Life without Love

A life without love
Is an empty vessel
A pond without fish
A house without warmth

To roam without destiny
To dream without vision
To follow fools without direction
To rhyme without reason

For I have walked an endless path
And I have danced to tepid song
And I have drunk a fruitless wine
And I take this lesson home

A life without love
Is no life at all

Six by Six

When holding out for better days
A thought to keep in mind
To negotiate a hidden maze
No matter what you find
Rise to ponder all you see
In a world beyond the me

A thought to keep in mind
While walking an untrodden road
Always seek the wayward kind
Avoid the devilish mode
To make a friend of all or none
Embrace the morning sun

To negotiate a hidden maze
Do not on sight rely
But walk as if in a daze
Until you think you'll cry
And wander through the forest pine
As if all is absolutely fine

No matter what you find
Regardless what you don't or do
When you're stuck in a tricky bind
Set your sites and see it through
If you ever seek another way
It may get you through the day

Rise to ponder all you see
Take it in and hash it over
If the answer still evades

Place your faith in four-leaf clovers
It's all random don't you see
Should it ever come down to me

In a world beyond the me
The sun will shine the moon will fall
A child will climb the tallest tree
And we will suffer through it all
We will dance and we will smile
As we will face another trial

Can I Remember?

(for Woody & Woodstock)

Can I remember?

Remember back to where I was this morning
On a park bench in the city
Where gray beards and tie-dyes
Took me back to Berkeley Square
Where hope and tension stirred the air
A woman with flowers smiled
Kissed my cheek and walked away
I wonder where she is today

Can I remember?

Remember back to yesterday
When thousands rushed the city square
We raised our voices strong in one
No more bombs no more war
No more killing in our name

Can I remember?

Iraq Iran and Vietnam
We marched the streets
A million strong
What happened to us?
Where are we now?

Can I remember?

Remember back to last week
No it's all the same
Nothing ever changes

We are the sum of our memories
Scattered like dry dust
In a hot summer breeze

Where are they now
When I need them
To comfort me

Thirty-One Poems

The obvious question: why?
The obvious rejoinder: why not?

Because it's there
Because we can
Because we've nothing
Better to do?

No one ever started a war
While writing poetry

Rhyme a dime
I would not pay a day
It has no meaning
Nor want of meaning
It is a passing phase
A way to while away the hours
And catch our thoughts astray

Like Ponce de Leon
We trap lightning in a jar
And pray it will outlast the moon

Who knows but that it will?

(make it 32)

Photos on the Mantel

Photos on the mantel
Memories of youthful grace
Children strike a pose and smile
Bright new clothes and delicate lace

Photos on the mantel
Memories of family joy
Chronicles of treasured moments
Pretty girls and strong young boys

Slivers here and there of sorrow
Trigger days of gloom
Cracks in the family portrait
Like prophecies of doom

We wear our history in the open
On our mantel for all to see
What's remembered what's forgotten
What we hide and what will be

Photos on the mantel
Don't look at them too long
Or they will hold you captive
Without regard for right or wrong

Silent Suffering

The mask of shame hides
The silent suffering of the victimized
Where is the shame of misfortune?
The homeless are not criminals
The addicted are not born immoral
The abused did not choose to be
The humble do not beg for favor
The proud do not howl in the streets
We are poor we are stricken
We are forgotten souls
That you do not see us suffer
Does not mean we don't exist

The Last Round (Old Muni)

I have walked these green highways
More times than I can count
I have grown to know each tree limb
every hollow mound break and slide

There are times when
I have bent the laws of physics
And times when I have
Crumbled in the wind

I have felt a brotherhood of purpose
Submitted to the will of nature
Ridden on the wings of hawks
Embraced the smallness of humanity
On these humble hallowed grounds

Seasons pass and we grow old
But one thing always stays the same
We laugh we cry we curse the sky
But we pay tribute to the game

Nothing lasts forever
So it is and so they say
But never ever could I believe
That time would reach this day

I remember my father and his pals
Buying drinks and sharing smiles
Telling stories till the sun goes down
We raise our glasses one and all:
To old Muni and one last round!

Save the Crow

Have we lived too long?
Have we done more harm than good?
How much are good intentions worth?
Save the tiger save the earth

We built guns and armies
Conquered people and took their land
We ripped the earth open to her core
And when she cried we dug for more

Did we know what we were doing?
When entire species disappeared?
Did we heed the many warnings
That this exactly is what we feared?

We never stopped to learn the lesson
Never listened never cared
To what the wise and learned know
What you reap is what you sew

Save the whale save the elephant
Save the bighorn sheep
Save the panther save the rhino
Save the tiger save the crow

A Day in Court

Forward he rose like a sullen sap
All bent with sorrow and regret
You stand accused of misplaced rage
Reading newspapers in public places
How do you plead?

I know the mayor your honor
If you please
Is there any way you can let this be?

We all make mistakes sir
We have our moments
This one sir is yours
Go your way

She bowed her head and gripped her
Hands like a penitent on holy ground
You stand accused of deliberate temptation
In full view of man and child
How do you plead?

If it pleases your majesty
I know the preacher's wife
She sends her love and lends her
Plea for kind consideration

Let the record show humility before
The court and sorrow thick as pudding
Meet me in the drawing room
And go your way

He rose alas in simple silence
To take his turn before the law
You stand accused of willful pride
And mocking men of dignity
How do you plead?

I am unjustly accused
A passing stranger in a foreign land
I know no one but me

Have you no contrition sir?
You strain our patience and defy
The court in all its pomp & circumstance
What's more you stain an almost perfect day
And test the legal limits of our mercy
Guilty! Guilty dark as sin!
Take him away!

Native Wisdom

They live in harmony with nature
And for this they are marked as heretics
They ask forgiveness for the kill
And for this they are considered fools

They bow to mother earth
Raise their hands to father sky
Give thanks to the great spirit
And for this they are branded savages

We have taken their sacred land
Slaughtered the buffalo
Declared war on their language
Banned their beliefs

But they were here a thousand years
Before the wasichu came
And a thousand years from now
They will be here still

Listen to your elders
Show respect for your fellow beings
Be honest and truthful
Do what is right
Treat the earth with kindness
And all creatures with dignity
Then may you find wisdom

When Death Comes Too Soon

Death comes for all in time
For the wicked and divine
For the blessed for the sinner
For the beloved and the kind

Like a shadow like a sigh
Or like lightning from a clear sky
She wraps her arms around us
And whispers: Time to die

Death can be merciful
When she ends a world of pain
When there is time to prepare
When our dark spirits are slain

Death will always be a mystery
Like the dark side of the moon
But the tragedy cuts deeper
When she comes for us too soon

Our tears flow in waves
Our hearts fill with sorrow
When a child of so much promise
Will not awaken in the morrow

(In Memoriam: Kobe & Gianna)

Beyond the Senses

To see without eyes
To hear without ears
Taste without tongue
Feel without touch
To smell beyond sensation

There is a world beyond the world
We smell touch taste see and hear
There is a universe expanding
There is a microcosmic sea
There is an underworld an overworld
A world of endless mystery

To spend a moment gazing
At the multitude of stars
Is to realize profoundly
How very small we are

For life is so much greater
Than what we know as fact
We would be fools to believe
It's no more than random acts

Vision

The world beyond our vision
Is greater than our view
If we see nothing but the visible
We are blinded to the truth

The lies of the heart
The sorrow in a smile
The glory of lesser conquest
To endure a solemn trial

Treasures lie behind the door
There are traps we do not see
There lie puzzles and mysteries
Beyond the farthest galaxies

Before you trust your sense of sight
Take a moment to reflect
For wisdom says and I believe
The heart is true the eyes deceive

Smell

Coyote sniffs the air to detect danger
Mammals large and small smell fear
The attentive prey escapes the kill
When a predator draws near

Dampened soil where fire burned
Sweat on a worried brow
The scent of liquid lovers
The breath of a salted sea
A rich cabernet or zinfandel
Catfish on an open flame
Your mother's cinnamon apples
Flowered plants in a lush garden
Coffee in the morning

Our lives are so enriched
By the intake of our nasal senses
Before we doubt we would do well
To appreciate our sense of smell

Hearing with the Heart

Hear the bells of the cathedral
As they linger in our memories
Feel them in our hearts
Long after the sound goes silent

Music transforms to dance
Dance is rhythmic vibration
We hear with our whole being
Waves of sound sensation

You can feel sorrow in the tears
of a child without crying
You can see rage in the face
of an angry man without yelling
You can rejoice in the dance
of inspired music
and sense the awesome force
of an unsettled sea without hearing

Turn off the volume from time to time
And listen with the heart

Touch

Solid as oak
Hard as an iron door
Smooth as ribbons of silk
Soft as a kitten's fur
Gentle as a cradle

If I had no sight to see your eyes
No tongue to taste your lips
If I could not smell your sweet perfume
Or hear your calming tone
The soothing joy of your gentle touch
Would be enough alone

Taste

Pesto pasta parmesan with pine nuts
And a sprinkling of lemon sauce
Deep red raspberry and oak aged wine
A hint of almond infused charcoal
Blueberry swirl with coconut cream

The senses sing at such delight
No need for hearing touch scent or sight

Taste of battle a hard-won fight
Taste of victory taste of spite
Tears of joy taste of sorrow
A taste lingering into tomorrow

The kind of taste that
Comes from the heart
Taste in fashion song and art

Everything that matters
Is a matter of taste

Loyalty

Loyalty is a delicate bond
It lasts no longer than a song
Whose sour note destroys the balance
And sends us tumbling for a fall

There is no loyalty in combat
When combatants take opposing sides
There is no trust when accusations
Are hurled like daggers to divide

How soon we cast away our friends
When we want a thing too much
Ambition is a toxic fiend
Poison to the touch

Beware to you who would betray
The knife will turn
The slayed will slay
And every dog will have its day

Friends and Brothers

Friends and brothers thick as blood
Sharing truths and finding kindness
When all the world is lost in blindness

We are the lucky ones
For we have made a choice
To walk the lonely paths of our lives
Alongside friends and brothers

So many miracles we've witnessed
So many wonders we've shared
We watch the sun go down and rise
Secure our bond will always thrive

We are brothers
We are friends
We stand together till the end

Golden Years

Ain't nothing gold about being old
The bones ache the muscles strain
Every day brings another pain

Something twists the fabric of time
A walk in the park the blink of an eye
Days weeks years fly by

Memories once lost are found
While the present slips away
We lose hold of solid ground
And live in yesterday

We are moved to sleep and dream
And sweet imagining for there
We can be whole again
There we are who we've always been
There we are ourselves

Gray is the color of the old
Slow wrinkled stumbling cold
But truth and wisdom lay here too
We grow old like worn out shoes

Ain't nothing else to say or do
We grow old like worn out shoes

Greed

What possesses men to take more
Than anyone could ever need?
How much is enough?
What accounts for greed?

Some collect memories like tumbleweeds
Some collect stars in a box
Some collect money titles and deeds
What accounts for greed?

Stealing food from the poor
To fatten a rich man's wallet
Take it all: a banker's creed
What accounts for greed?

So much obsession for things
So little time for people
Don't they wonder where it leads?
There's no account for greed

Antiques

A hundred years ago
When a chair was meant to last
A hundred years
A skilled hand
Combined with sharp tools
To carve exquisite lines
In hard oak

A hundred years ago
A table meant to last
A hundred years
Took form from raw timber
Shaped and varnished
With the tender care
Of master craftsmen

A hundred years ago
When tables chairs
Desks and cabinets
Were works of art
Designed to leave
A mark for posterity

A hundred years ago
They cared
Today we buy
Furniture in boxes
And assemble them
At home

Artist in Society

Art is real
Art is magic
Art is love passion truth and beauty
Art is everything most admirable
About the human race

There is no greater pursuit in life
Than to create works of art
Products of illusive imagination
Transformations of the heart

Applications of light and shadow
Blends of vivid color
Tones that no one else can hear
Words divinely inspired

Weaving stories that warm the soul
Teaching eyes to see new patterns
Ears to hear new melodies
Building structure out of anarchy
Destroying sense of order
Carving marble into mythology
Shaping desire with common hands

Art is the medicine that cures disease
The artist as healer and alchemist

Artists will live as long as breath sustains
Art will live forever

Miracles

Imbedded in everything that breathes
Everything that lays within our vision or
Beyond our view

Hummingbirds and honeybees
Laughing dogs and dancing trees
Engaging books and vivid dreams
Growing up to become for instance me

Miracles beyond our comprehension
In every particle of being
Dendrites spark and stars explode
In distant galaxies
Minds collide and ideas divide
Into a million constellations

There are no small miracles
Only small minds

Numbers

(for Spalding Gray)

There was a man who saw numbers everywhere
In the city in the desert in the invisible air
One for self two for opposites
Three for transcendental thinking
Four solid walls five common senses
Six wasted decades seven waves to destiny

There was a man who counted numbers
He swam to Cambodia counting every stroke

Eight infinite possibilities
Nine the number divine

Swimming to Cambodia takes a lot of time
Counting to Cambodia fills the mind

Ten wanton murders
Eleven sickened saints

A more brilliant mind was never wasted
But let's not be unkind
Who's to say what counts and what
Does not? Not I

There was a man who counted himself
Among the dead
I count him among the ones
I most admired

Brotherhood of Age

We used to talk about sports and politics
Now we talk about maladies and medications
Swollen arches aches and pains

A former president once speculated
How quickly our differences would vanish
If we were attacked by an alien race

How quickly our differences vanish now
With common ailments high blood pressure
Rheumatoid arthritis irregularity
Inevitable mortality

The brotherhood of age is a curiosity
Founded on infirmity its bond holds
Strong and true like yin and yang
Like super glue

We are brothers now and always
Together to the end of time

Mama Wandered

Reliable all her life
When everything around her lost control
Mama held steady

But she wandered in her later years
She saw faces in the shadows
Monsters in the dark
And she ran like anyone would do
She wandered in the night
To escape her demons

Someone always took her home
With a solemn smile
She never had to face her ghosts alone

In quiet times she would confess
They are not real
They are phantoms
Creations of a worried mind

And yet they weighed on her
Played with her fears
Tipped the balance at times

She saw and heard them
Cold and real as right
She felt their presence
And so she wandered
In the lonely night

The Human Touch

(Friends on Facebook)

In the modern world
We have no need of human contact
We talk to machines
They give us what we want
The machines talk back to us
We yell at them and tell them secrets
No one else can hear
But I remember humankind
And sometimes sense them drawing near

Comes a time to lose what we abuse
A time to rediscover what is dear
When we reach out and no one answers
We will have realized our fear

Friends on Facebook mean so much
And yet we miss the human touch

Pray we can return
Before that bridge is burned

Woodstock

Time unfolds on memories of Woodstock:

Sunrise

Farmland in upstate New York
Becomes the stuff of dreams
A chapter in history
A story of mythology
Immortalized on film

Sunset

Memories warped in time
History redefined
Anarchy and narcissism
Indulgence and shameless sin
(without shame there is no sin)

Moonrise

A dream of freedom realized
A rising of the human spirit
A balance of disparate souls
A place where the better nature
Of humanity flourished
A bonding in music and dance
Nirvana peace of mind
A magical mystical ride

To those who remember never doubt
Woodstock was a singular place
In time

Hard Times

I been doing some hard travelin'
I thought you knowed...

I hear that Woody Guthrie tune
Near every time I hit the road
The loneliest highway in America
A lonesome valley named Shenandoah
In the heartland of old Virginia
A university dorm in New Hampshire
Where the old man of the mountain
Looked down on us
A place to lay my head and rest
My weary mind in Omaha
Down to my last dollar in Albuquerque
Stranded on the interstate in Winnemucca
Selling vacuums to make the rent
Picking peaches and tangerines
Singing songs for shelter
Needing a job so bad
I almost sold my soul

I been doing some hard travelin'
Way down the road...

Ran out of gas on a lonesome highway
Slept in a public park
Caught a ride in the nick of time
Drove through a hailstorm
In tornado alley

Hard times are some of the best times
I ever had

Good Times

Remember the good times
Acknowledge the bad

The time you learned to drive a stick
The first time you played and won
The time she asked you to stay
The feeling you had when she smiled

Moments in a life that fill you with joy
Taking in an ocean breeze
Hearing a song that makes you cry
Embracing a child with a sigh

Collect them like treasures
And hold them apart
For the times that you need them
To comfort your heart

Remember the moment you understood
Acknowledge the bad
Remember the good

Westside

I grew up on the west side of town
Where the poor people live
Black white yellow brown

Lived worked played together
Learned to get along
Through all kinds of weather

Race riots back in 65
Homelessness and crime
We were lucky to get out alive

Depression recession
It was all the same
We understood early on
We were pawns in the game

We went through it all
Didn't care what they say
What we failed to learn then
We're still learning today

Cool Baby Blue

(Memories of D'Arc Underground)

Cool baby blue ocean breeze
If you've got the cure
I want the disease

Slide baby slide
Play that old guitar
Seal it on up
Take it home in a jar

Sing baby sing
Make the old man moan
Ain't nobody preaching
Without sins to atone

Pray baby pray
We all like it that way
Make it last all night
And half through the day

Cool

Thelonious Monk is cool beyond cool
A sunny day in February
Cry of the hawk in spring
Caw of the canyon crow

Brambu Drezi cool as cool goes
Drumbeat of a tribal reunion
Endless forest of sequoia pine
A newborn's internal glow

Petty and the Heartbreakers
Knowledge of a spirit guide
The scent of clear clean water
A walk down the boulevard slow

Beyoncé meets Billie Holiday cool
A song so smooth it flows
The grace of a ballerina
A secret nobody knows

It's a thing no one can teach
You have it or you don't
If you're lucky you were born with it
Embedded in your soul

Beyond

What lies beyond the last glimmer of light?
Beyond the hazy lazy dreams of summer
Beyond the long lonesome highway
The last gas station
End of the line

What lies beyond the edge of the universe?
The black hole of an open mind
The prayers of the sainted
A glimpse of divine

What lies beyond the darkness?
Do strange beings dwell there?
Is there warmth to comfort us?
Or fearful spirits to despair?

What lies beyond the deepest deep?
Are there answers that make us whole?
That unravel the impenetrable
And settle in our souls

Cynicism of Youth

I was not born a cynic
I learned to doubt
She captured me while I was sleeping
Followed me on lonely journeys
Enveloped me in moments of despair
Chased me down alleyways
And pressed me to a wall of stone

The more I fought
The more she held me down
The more I suffered
The more she pressed me to the ground

I learned the art of cynicism
From those who knew her well
Friends who were never friends
Lovers who betrayed

I fell in love for a spell
Reading Nietzsche and O'Neill
Wearing darkness as a veil

I brooded like the poets
Like a rebel without a cause
I reveled in my loneliness
Defying norms and normal laws

Only when I surrendered
Did she leave me alone
She didn't like my happiness
She didn't like my tone

Mirrors

Take away the mystery
Make me see the truth
Unveil my darkest memories
The secrets of my youth

If you look into the mirror
And you don't like what you find
Learn to love all others
See the good in humankind

Only then will you reflect
Only then can you embrace
The beauty that you see
The goodness in your face

Mirror mirror on the wall
Who's the wisest of them all
Not I for I have peeked beneath
And I have glimpsed the fall

For mirrors lie and flatter
And hide the truth that matters
When all is said and done
We are all of us but one

The Fighter

When you want it so bad
You can taste it in your dreams
When it defines who and what you are
When it gets down to wrong and right
Comes a time you have to fight

There are times to walk away
To keep the peace
Save it for another day
There are times to keep it light
And there are times to stand and fight

When a child is in the line of fire
When innocence is at stake
When decency demands it
When doing nothing would disgrace
When all options are exhausted
When fighting back's the only way

When justice is within your sight
Stand your ground and fight

The Untold Story

I had a friend who might have been
The funniest man on earth

The life of every party
A song and dance man
He had stories about everything
And every story had a punchline
Except his own

That story he never told

Looking back it makes me wonder
What sorrows might have dwelled within
The jokes the laughs the crooked smile
That knowing telling grin

What dark secrets did he hold
In the story he never told

(for Mike)

The Awkward Age

The age when it almost hurts to talk
And you can feel the eyes of others
Watching as you trip on the sidewalk

Mind expands in fits and bursts
Body grows at lightning speed
No matter how much you consume
You can never get what you need

It's the age when you desperately
Want to belong
The age when everything
That can goes wrong

But worry not my young friend
It will come to a merciful end
And you will look back bemused
At the awkward age that so abused

Ghosts

His ghosts descend to suck out the light
Like a brood of vampires on a moonlit night
Doubt grips him by the neck and will not let go
Haunted by what he does not know

He is lonely in a crowd
He looks within he looks around

Sanctuary he cries aloud!
To no one within hearing
This pain belongs to everyone
Why must I suffer alone?

Aimlessly he walks the streets
In sadness and despair
And everywhere he wanders
Dogs bark and children stare
They see what others cannot see
His spirits fill the air
He pleads with them to leave him be
Or let their secrets show

They laugh and mock his desperate pleas
For what he does not know

Another Time

I might have been a saint
Or a master of crime
If only I was born
In another place and time

I should have been an actor
An artist or a mime
Had only I been born
In another space in time

A merchant in ancient Rome
A knight on a crusade
A courtesan in Paris
A soldier in Madrid

A pilot a dancer a madman a king
The truth is in dreams
I have been all these things

A Certain Age

At a certain age (I'll never tell)
You begin to wonder

How many years how many tears
How many days and minutes remain
How many seasons of flowers in bloom
How many walks in the light of the moon
How many dreams about dying in vain

How many sunsets on a calm western sky
How many cheers at a baseball game
How many chances to call out a lie
How many moments of glory or shame

Life guarantees nothing
From the moment we're born
Not a breath not an instant
Nor a sparkling new morn

Our lives are a journey
From beginning to end
The last click of the clock
We cannot know when

Rich Man Poor

Poor man waits on tables
Wades through mud
Wages hours sweat and blood

Rich man feeds on plenty
Has no cares
Homes and castles everywhere

Poor man counts his pennies
Savors time
Wonders how to make it rhyme

Rich man towers up above
Dreams of love
Never has to push or shove

Rich or poor do they not bleed
No indeed
The one man wants the other needs

Universal Mind

The seed of all religions
Is the universal mind
It springs from contemplation
Over a bottle of fine wine

William Blake and Joseph Campbell
Are masters of this thought
The immortal soul of mortal man
Is a thing that can't be bought

Who doubts the proposition that
Poetic genius is divine
But it cannot breach the mystery
Of the universal mind

Innocence

When the world was perfect
Before the cold hand of hardship
Or the hot hand of desire
Pressed down upon the mind
Like the first drop of blood
From an open wound

When life was pure
And there was no one better than
Smarter than deeper than stronger
Or more precious than
Your mother's dearest child

When the universe was in your hands
Before the fall before the flood
Before the first objection
Rejection or correction

When life existed for your pleasure
Like the center of a storm

The Missing Wheel

Candles without moonlight
Halloween with fright
Love without affection
On a long lonely night

The Doors without Morrison
Big Brother without Joplin
Experience without Hendrix
The Dead without Garcia
Garcia without the Dead
Like butter without bread

Rock and roll without the beat
The train don't roll without being led

No man or woman can stand alone
Against the hard winds of oppression
We march together or not at all
To bring the movement home

We can reach the farthest destiny
When every person plays their part
But if one wheel is missing
We won't get past the start

After the Fall

After the fall you pick yourself up
And get back in the game
After the fall you find out
What substance you're made of

If you're made of cotton candy
Stay down for the count
Nothing matters and no one
Cares what you're about

If you're made of stronger stuff
Grab your tail and pick it up
We all take a shot or two
What matters is what next you do

Turn your back and walk away
Come back to fight another day

Plant your staff and hold your ground
Don't let the stumbles get you down

Be proud march on and if you fall
Get right back up and stand tall

You can't control what others do
What you can control is you

Family

The father the mother the sacred child
What divides the civilized from the brutish wild
Is family

We are born to blood acquire friends
Family sticks beginning to end
With friends and loved ones
We learn to fly
With family we live and die

There are times that test the strongest ties
When bitter fades our love will rise
To comfort us the endless night
To bend the darkness toward the light

Earth

This water filled wonderland of plenty
This magnificent garden exploding with life
This spinning sphere hurtling through
Space at unimaginable speed
This home to uncountable species
This birthplace to art religion and
Infinite variations of thought
This liquid ball of stone and molten core
This symphony of endless mystery
This miracle of perpetual paradox
This paradise of plenty
This wondrous earth

Wind

Winds howling in a raging sky
Hard times looming by and by
Storm brewing in the deep blue sea
Winds of change through tall trees

Winds of destruction coming round
Bending towers till they hit the ground
Gales the world will not forget
Horrific payback for karmic debt

The wind is the voice of our mother
It springs from the clear blue air
Touching every sister brother
Defy her if you dare

Fire

Flames strike horror on a peaceful night
Wildlife scatters owls take flight
The mind rejects this awful sight
The sorrow awaiting morning's light

Lives destroyed loved ones lost
To live in paradise at such a cost
They cleared a forest and built a town
Destined one day to be burned down

Homes churches city hall
The fire came and took them all
The people build their town again
And surround it with a wall

A madness born of hope and prayer
This lightning cannot strike again
It can and will you can be certain
And it will lower the final curtain

(in memory of the Paradise fire)

Water

The waters rise to swallow the land
And the masses wonder why
Precious water brings the gift of life
Why must so many people die?

You poison rivers torch the sky
And now you dare to wonder why
You take what you have given
You reap what you have sown

We lived our lives in ignorance
From blissful night to morning
Never thinking what might happen
Never listening to the warnings

So now we face the consequence
Of our own willful negligence
We must restore the water
We must renew the air

That is unless we just don't care

Kids

A great man once said
A kid will throw down a ten-dollar toy
To play with a cardboard box
Time was that was true
Not any more
Now kids spend their money
At the electronic game store

I'm not complaining it's what kids do
But I hope they see what's right and true

We're handing them a world of trouble
We can only pray they get it right
Undo what we have done
And keep the dream within their sight

It takes commitment imagination
Sacrifice to right what we did wrong

We can only apologize

We're sorry for the precedent
We're sorry for the money spent
We're sorry for all the wars
We're sorry for closed doors
We're sorry for all we did
And what we didn't do
We're relying on you kids
To set it right and see it through

A Silence of the Soul

There are views that steal your breath away
There are works of art so stunning
Their subjects seem to glow
But there is no greater beauty than
A silence of the soul

Northern lights in a sky of a million stars
The smile that makes you whole
An act of kindness in a world of woe
The moment Ulysses arrives back home

A lotus flower in a lily pond
Knowing that you'll never be alone
A song that plays the heart strings
And strikes harmonic tones

An exploding sunset an infant's laugh
The blooming of a rose
A dream of wingless flight
More valuable than gold

But there is no greater beauty than
A silence of the soul

Beauty is as beauty does as everybody knows
But there is no greater beauty than
A silence of the soul

The Old Actor

His voice still rumbles when he takes the stage
Though it stumbles now and then
In deference to his age

His presence like a beast still commands all eyes
As he raises his hands and doffs his disguise
An actor among actors a man among men
He played every role and some he played again

Once more unto the breach! the saying goes
God for Harry England and Saint George!

I am a man more sinned against than sinning
Blow winds and crack your cheeks! he cries

Once more he bows and teases
The audience to rise

Once more before we say goodbye

Good People

We are so polarized
In our politics our bent of mind
In how we see the world
And how we wish the world could be

There are more ways to divide
Than stars in a Sierra sky

I have known good people of all kinds
Who do not share my point of view
I have worked with them talked with them
Enjoyed with them a drink or two

In the end it comes down to this:
We are more the same than differing
We want what's right and true
We all want what we are due

Color us white black brown or blue
We want to know what we should do

Father and Son

A father tells his son
Life is fair
You get what you need

A son asks his father
Then why is it so hard
To succeed?

A father tells his son
Never give up
Keep trying

A son asks his father
How many times must I try
The same thing over and over?

A father tells his son
I don't have all the answers

A son asks his father
Who does?

The Balance

There is a time to go bold
There is a time to go slow
Too little leaves us wanting
Too much takes its toll

In the great expanse of history
We've swung east and west
But when the final vote is counted
Balance is the test

So take the long perspective
If you want to sleep at night
Have we swung too far left
Or have we drifted too far right?

Only time will tell the story
Of a nation so divided
It turned so far in one direction
The error could not be righted

The Storyteller

The old woman sat back in her rocking chair
Picked up her knitting needles
And prepared to tell a story

Firelight shined in her eyes
Spreading warmth and illumination
To every corner of the room

The children leaned forward
Anticipating her first words
Words that would signal a journey
Into a land of magical beings
Two steps beyond imagination

She had taken them so many places
Too many to remember

A deep dank cave where rabid eyes
Sprang from moss covered walls

A mystical forest where blooming
Flowers spoke in twisted rhymes
Where trees formed towering bridges
To starlit castles in an azure sky

A domed city where the working poor
Were doomed to live and die outside

A backward village where people
Slept by day and worked by night

So many worlds where good beats evil
Where brutes are thwarted by the kind

So many worlds to open a child's fresh mind

Each child by instinct knew these moments
Would be treasured till the end of time

End of the Day

At the end of the day we sit in our rockers
Looking out at a world gone by
Looking out at the world we leave behind
As the world looks back at us in wonder

One man sees civilization in decline
Another sees a nation rising

I see a world of great promise
A generation of enlightened youth
An army of dedicated activists
An energy that cannot be denied

But I also see a world of destruction
Democracy disintegrating glaciers melting
A tortured land a rising sea
Poisoned water and toxic air
Natural beauty that no longer will be

At the end of the day
We view our walk through time
from a place of solitude
through solitary eyes
A place of hope and sorrow
Knowing full well
we may not greet tomorrow

Highs and Lows

When the highs are so high
The infinite universe cannot contain them
The lows so low the deepest depths
Of the deep blue sea are but shallow

We ride the tides like surfers
On the edge of oblivion
Worshipping the gods of adventure
Ever seeking the rush of adrenaline
Never worrying about the fall

But the fall must come
And the sorrow invades every particle
Of being and every story brings a waterfall
Of tears and darkness shrouds the endless night

Find a balance

We cannot survive a rollercoaster
Ride that never ends

Find a balance

Life has its ups and downs
But we must plant our feet
On solid ground and pray
The morning comes

When I Go

Don't cry for me when I go
Laugh sing share a tale or two
Then lift a glass and let it show
But let there be no tears of woe

Let it be said I was a man
Of simple wants and deep passion
My good outweighed my flaws
Let it be said I traveled a long hard road
Made a friend or two along the way
Pleased some angered others
Always fought against injustice
Stood with my sisters and brothers

So lift a glass and let it show
But don't cry for me when I go

Vengeance

Base instinct raw emotion
The beast of vengeance lives
Within our beating hearts
Struggling to break free
And wreak havoc on the world

Vengeance is the cause of small minds
And the fuel of endless wars

Vengeance feeds revenge
Until the cycle of destruction
Thrives in perpetuity

There is no greater evil than
The desire and the need to make
The other suffer more than
Oneself

Uncle Henry

(for Henry Miller)

Uncle Henry was the coolest cat on the
Planet for any number of years

The man cruised the tropics collecting
Women and followers like a man on a
Mission like a devotee on a cause

Paris and Manhattan were the only cities
Big enough cool enough sophisticated enough
To call his home

Anais was his muse and inspiration
Until she threatened the grand divinity
Of his journey with her own

He settled in a forest of towering redwoods
To become a guru a bodhisattva
A contemplative master of living in peace
And harmony with all beings

Uncle Henry was the coolest cat on the
Planet for any number of years

Joltin' Joe

He was the luckiest man in creation
For as long as it lasted

He was the toast of all New York
Man of the hour
Drinks with the chairman
Dinner with the mayor
Respect of every man who ever
Played the game and every woman
Who ever watched him play

Then he met a woman who towered
Over his life like a statue in celluloid

He held onto her as long as he could
Then he let go
He had to let go
She was a drowning woman
Six feet down and sinking
And he was only a man
Only a ballplayer
A hero to many
But only a man

He could not save her
So he let her go

Every year for two decades of sorrow
He put roses on her grave

Uncle Arthur

(for Arthur Miller)

He wrote the story of America
The American Dream
The American Nightmare
The last frontier to the Salem witch trials

He wanted to rescue America's sweetheart
From the depraved idolaters that swirled
Around her till she could not breathe

He thought he could write a happy
Ending for them both
Alas he could not write
What was already written

A tragic tale of jealousy envy
Abandonment and betrayal

It was a story so painful not even he
Had the heart to write it

Forgetting

Forgot my keys
Forgot my wallet
Forgot my credit card
Forgot where I parked my car

Forgot my number
Forgot my destiny
Forgot my message
Forgot who or what you are

If we live long enough we arrive at a point
Where we realize we've forgotten
More than we will ever learn

It's not sad but it seems so
There is great virtue in forgetting
Forgetting is forgiving without effort
There is mercy in forgetting
We let go all shortcomings
Ghosts and tragedies

Just as fading sight spares us the gradual
Deterioration of our appearance
So our fading memories spare us the
Reality of our deteriorating minds

When we have forgotten all that was
And all that is pray we remember love
In the end it's all that matters

The Canyon

In all my life
In all my journeys and adventures
The one place on the planet
That puts me in a place of awe
Is the Grand Canyon

In all my life
The Canyon is the one place
That enables me to believe
All things are possible

That humanity can rise up
In unity and peace
That we can learn to respect
The earth and all living things
That weapons of mass destruction
Can be banned and destroyed
That the sun can power the world
That all people can be treated
With the respect they deserve
That our spirits can soar
Like the eagle touching the sky
That everything we imagine
Can become reality

Mitakuye oyasin
Let it be so

Money

For the love of money
We become lesser beings

We build towers through the clouds
Obliterate the sky
Bow down to money masters
And pretend we don't know why

For the love of money
We lower ourselves on the scale
And empower the obscene wealthy
To become the obscene elite

We are equal in value and rights
No one should ever put themselves down
Because they don't have money
Or raise themselves up because they do

Wherever power leads
Money is close behind
Whenever power bleeds
Money falls in line

The Muse

An artist dreams of a muse
To stir his creative juices
He obsesses night and day
Till the muse must go away

For a love that burns too strong
Must never last too long
And every artist must learn
To let go a love that burns

The artist consumes his muse
And moves on to another
But what of the muse?
Must she live to serve others?

I have known many muses
Who are not what they seem
What if the muse is the artist
And the artist is the dream?

Shame

What is shame if not
desire's punishment?

To desire shame is to defy
The law of gravity
And hasten to thy grave

There can be no shame
Save that which we impose
Upon ourselves

Therefore to feel shame
Is to desire shame
And that is neither right
Nor natural

Sir have you no shame?
No sir I have none

I have more than I need
Would you like some of mine?

I am neither so righteous
Nor so divine

Keep your shame and hold it close
For there may come a time
When you need it more than most

(Humbly for William Blake)

Prayer for a Giving Man

There is not now nor ever has been
A person more kind and giving
Than my brother and my friend

He might not ask for himself
So for those who love him
And those who care
I offer this my humble prayer

Let him live a long and fruitful life
May he always possess his creative drive
May he always listen to his heart
And may he live to see his grandchild
Grow up and thrive

(for Bob)

North

Wanderer where will you go?

North is a place of shivering cold
But it casts a stunning light
With layers of shimmering ice and snow
To calm your spirit on a winter's night

The northern winds blow hard and strong
With piercing logic and sober reason
To cool the overheated passions of those
Who thrive on chaos and treason

Go north to soothe your soul
Go north to ponder mysteries
Go north to find the truth within
Go north and tell the world to cease

You are your own being
At peace with who you are
Unafraid to walk alone
And trace your own north star

South

Wayfarer where will you go?

South is where it all began
And where it comes to final rest
The sultry south the birth of man
A mother's womb a woman's breast

Go south to unravel your emotions
Reveal the contents of your heart
Unleash your passion and devotion
Find a way to live apart

Southern winds are warm and true
They can bring you to your knees
But they can also soothe your soul
Like a gentle summer breeze

Go south to sing your heart song
Your soft and tender side
Go south to ease the suffering
And learn how to abide

East

Truth seeker where will you go?

The east is the springboard of knowledge
Sculptures monuments architectural design
From ancient seers to modern philosophers
Immortal beauty and wonders divine

Go east to seek your destiny
Go east to trace your line
Go east to find the answers
That challenge a searching mind

The eastern winds bring a frightful chill
That stuns and makes the heart go still
But while the mind may be inspired
The soul is unfulfilled

Go east to learn and study
If knowledge is what you need
To gather from the masters
Go east to plant the seed

West

Adventurer where will you go?

The west is where all life is laid to rest
Where the sun dissolves into the sea
Where we confront our final test
Where what we are is what will be

Go west for new beginnings
Go west to find the line
Between your wish and your desire
Go west or be left behind

The western winds blow hot and cold
To challenge when you're young
And comfort when you're old
Go west to break the mold

Go west to meet your maker
And enjoy your final hours
To breathe your final breaths
And collapse like wilting flowers

Pressure

Every second of every minute of
Every hour of every day
Like a dagger to the gut
A pain that never goes away

The walls close in like a
Twisted executioner's vice
You want relief more than life
But that you cannot entice

Kindness is distorted and false
Everyone you encounter is wrong
Your stomach tied in knots
Your heart pounding like a bass drum

Like an overheated boiler
Like a dam overrun
You can feel impending doom
An explosion yet to come

Is there nothing that can end this misery?
Is there nothing that can still this dull
Pounding ache in the walls of my skull?
Is there no one who can lift the spell?

Go now leave me alone
While I crawl into a cave
And hide for a hundred years

Mourning

Our loved ones fall like trees in a storm
We suffer grieve shed tears and mourn
Our memories cannot satisfy our souls
The hollow place within our hearts
Becomes a gaping hole

The immortal tragedy of life
That every one of us must die
That our loved ones must suffer
Sure as stars in an endless sky

There is no other way but through
But knowing this may comfort you
The days of sorrow will someday end
And we will smile and laugh again

The Families

We came from different sides of the river
Divided by the railroad tracks
Different cultures and traditions
Different ways of seeing things

The untimely death of a loved one
Someone no one could foresee
Brings us together in remembrance
For we are family

There is more here than bloodline
There is empathy and love
We possess the same ambitions
Look to the same spirits above

For one spirit guides us all
On that we all agree
We nod and acknowledge
We are family

It may seem simple even cliché
But it sounds a clarion call
What binds us together is everything
What divides is nothing at all

Racing the Clock

At a certain age we feel a rush
As life presses forward from behind
In the marrow of our bones we feel
What once existed only in our minds

To know each moment could be our last
Not as an abstraction but a stone-cold fact
Alters perception of everything we see
Testing the limits of what can and cannot be

It's a race against time that we cannot win
Like living a life without the stain of sin
One more poem or story one more telling line
O lord let me drink just one more glass of wine

But time marches on while we stumble through
The final divination: we haven't a clue
So take it easy old friend and enjoy the ride
It doesn't matter what you leave
It's what you hold inside

Humility

Stand on the ledge of Grand Canyon
On a clear shining day
Behold the expansive sky from the height
Of Donner's Pass at midnight
Feel the waves of a warm Pacific coast
Wash over you at sunrise
Absorb the beauty of a single work
Of art in the moment of inspiration

The sum total of all we learn
Comes down to this:

In the face of all we know
Lies the body of what we do not know
Temper your confidence with a good
Measure of doubt
Knowing that humility comes
With the wisdom of age

Graeagle

Tucked into the high Sierras
A village born of hard-working folk
Hunting fishing solid as granite
They worked hard for a living until
The money men came

Overnight the tourists took hold
The locals moved to the back of the bus
Country clubs and gated communities
Vacation manors restaurants and pubs

Paradise paved and monetized
Nothing remains the way it was
The constant is constant change
Hold on to the memories

The hawk still lands on the tall pines
The eagle still glides in the high sky
Deer still gather in fields of grass
And old timers still tell stories
Of how it used to be

Tragedy

Pestilence and plague across the globe
The rumble of a San Andreas quake
A chain of twisters through tornado alley
Oceans rise to swallow the land

Levees give way on the lower ninth
Nuclear meltdown radioactive waste
A man with issues and an automatic gun
Pile up on the interstate

Tragedy is a part of life
We roll with it as it rolls over us
We learn to look away
There is only so much heartbreak
We can take
There are only so many tears
To cleanse our shaken souls

We will abide
We will endure
We will reach back
Shake it off
And move on

Comedy

A clown trips and almost falls
An old man tries in vain
To open someone else's car
A dog and a preacher walk into a bar
Barump bump

We find humor where none should be
We laugh at harmless tragedy
A stutter a stammer a stumble a fall
We dig for the humor beneath it all

The human spirit was born to laugh
And dwell in the halls of joy
For though we cast long dark shadows
In our hearts we're still girls and boys

Give

There are times when all seems lost
The endless sorrow exacts a cost
There are limits to what we each can bear
Past which we dare no longer care

And yet we give all that we can
The giving nature of woman and man
We witness need and we lend a hand
We see madness we seek to understand

In the final hours before the fall
Let the word go out to one and all
He gave more than he had to give
He'd give more now if he could live

The Climb

The slow climb up the mountain side
Each step a death defying ride
But to those who seek to reach the top
There is no choice we cannot stop

We fix our sites and set our minds
To all distractions we are blind
We will not quit until we find
The destiny we're looking for
A goal a mark a certain score
Once achieved we'll look for more

We are the driven the ones who seek
We are not cautious we are not meek
The ones they call adventure freaks
We never settle we always lead
We are the first to plant the seed
The climb holds everything we need

(We keep on climbing until we bleed)

Stray Memories

The fading mind takes hold of stray
Memories like lifelines to the soul

The smile of a stranger
A moment of clarity
A slip of the tongue
The shake of a hand
A sudden embrace
An explosion of rage

Thoughts like flickering light
Memories in flight

A collapse in sorrow
A mother's tears
A burst of glory
A dance on ice

They tap the mind and slip away
They leave a mark but will not stay
And cannot vow to return someday

The Soul

The essential self
The being in being human
The great unknown
The infinite mystery

It bears many names
In many cultures and religions
It is known to all yet remains
Unknowable beyond understanding

The eternal core
The guiding principle
The endless drive
The beating heart
The constant yearning

It is the all and nothing at all
It is the unifying force and
The mark of individuality
It is the thing without which
Nothing matters

Transcendent Love

The young man craves romantic love
Sensual sexual erotic love

But when we grow older
And the die is cast
We desire a sturdier mold
The kind of love that will last

The young man seeks the stars
The old man stands on earth
The young man breaks his heart
The old man knows love's worth

To love itself is to transcend
To fix one's star to something
greater than oneself

The Simple Life

We live our lives from day to day
Working long and hard for little pay
The simple life or so they say
Is not so simple but it's our way

We press on from night to night
We keep our families within our sight
We don't ask for help or special favors
We have no use for fools or saviors

Tough as leather hard as stone
A proud people down to the bone
The strongest stock you've ever known
We only ask to be left alone

We mind our own business
We take care of our kin
We keep a tight circle
On the ones within

The Kids are Alright

Past the age of need
They do what they want
Talk when they feel like it
And keep to themselves
More often than not

They are shedding their innocence
Day by day hour by hour
They are letting the world in
They are keeping the world out
They are building faith
They are shedding doubt

They are becoming themselves
Estranged from who and what they were
They are finding their place
Marking a path and planting
Their first steps

We look back with longing
For the days of simple pleasures
And simple truths

We belong to the past
The future belongs to youth

Metropolis

Walking the trail of towers
In the echoes of my memories
I feel a crushing burden
Of eyes avoiding mine

Belonging to a monster so immense
Brings a certain sense of pride
To step where countless steps were
Planted so many times before
Makes you stop and breathe the magic
Makes you wonder what's in store

To live in the metropolis
And never see the sun
Makes you wonder what you're missing
And you'll miss it when it's done

In Dreams

In dreams we live alone
In the company of others
We have no want of things
No father and no mother

We are free to fall or rise
According to our will
We can seek true wisdom
Or we can seek another thrill

We can wander through the stars
We can answer every call
We can bathe ourselves in pleasure
Or we can deny it all

If you want to know your self
Who you were and who you are
Observe yourself in dreams
And mark your guiding star

(Crazy Horse was right
We live in dreams
In waking life we die)

The Buffalo

A magnificent beast
It roamed the plains for millennia
Before the white eyes came with their
Long horned cattle that uprooted wild grass
And left the land barren like the
White man's soul

An ancient creature
It could not exist confined by fencing
And barbed wire that ripped its flesh
And blocked the path of migration
To the great wandering herds

A noble animal
That formed the core of a noble culture
That provided sustenance food clothing
Shelter and lived in harmony with all
Earthbound beings before the age
Of rapid decline

The buffalo
We slaughtered them to the edge of
Extinction but they rose from the dead
To reclaim the great majestic plains
Once more

Mitakuye Oyasin

The white the red the living the dead
We are all one the Lakota said
Two leg four leg six leg eight
As we share the planet we share its fate

Creatures of the air land and sea
Majestic mountains deserts plains
We breathe the same air
We drink the same water
We possess the same needs

We are connected in every way
When we bless the soaring hawk
We are blessed
When we praise another
We lift ourselves
When we harm another
We are forever injured
When we take life
Life is taken from us

We are one

Used Books

Some go to parks or shopping centers
Antique or sporting goods shops
My father went to bookstores
Used bookstores where you could
Smell the wisdom of accumulated volumes

As a child I wandered through the towers
Of knowledge dazzled and bemused
There's nothing like the scent of old books

As a child I thought it was the smell of
Decaying words decaying thoughts
The decline of civilization

I knew then I wanted to contribute
To the towers of collected works of art
And science the grand parade of printed
Works the cathedral of secret letters

When I heard the phrase
Man of letters I knew
That was who
I wanted to be

And so I am

The Right to be Wrong

We inform the world what we have found
We declare our truths loud and strong
We pick our facts and stand our ground
We proclaim the right to be wrong

If we believe in democracy
The sacred power of the vote
We cannot pick and choose results
We cannot skip the sour notes

Despite our best intentions
There are times we are profoundly wrong
It is then we must bite our tongues
Sound our protests but go along

We have the right to free speech
We have the right to vote our choosing
We have the right to sing a dissonant song
And we have the right to be wrong

Space

I have dreamed
of floating in space
since the day humanity
chose the day
of my birth
to walk on the moon

I have dreamed
of traveling across
the great expanse
having no weight
walking on air
defying gravity
exploring new worlds
testing the limits
of common man
for as long as
memory serves me

I have yearned
to slip through the coils
of time to distant galaxies
where alien beings
share knowledge
and experience
with lowly humans
like me

Alas such dreams
and desires have escaped
my life span

on a planet doomed
to expiration
before advancing
past its infancy

Seven Ages

Born in the age of innocence
Grew up in the age of awakening
Matured in the age of enlightenment
Endured the age of indulgence
Marked time in the age of compromise
Rose up in the age of challenges
Broke down in the age of reckoning

A life well lived as the poet said
Driven by love wherever it led

Sadie Mae

She spoke to me with her eyes
The moment we walked into the room
A hall of cages for abandoned dogs

She pulled me to her
And touched my soul

Her name was Sadie Mae
It broke my heart when I had
To leave her that day
Papers to be sorted
Decisions to be made

We pulled her out of purgatory
The following afternoon

She remained by my side
The rest of her life
Always loyal always giving
Always telling me what to think
What to feel and what to do

She was almost always right
And she was never wrong
And man she sure could sing a song
I hear her now and always will
She made my heart go still

I loved that dog

I cried when I had to let her go

She was the best dog I ever knew
A whole lot better than humans too

I miss my Sadie Mae
I miss her every night and day

The Circle

If life is a circle
Then life becomes a race
To its completion

If the circle becomes a line
And wanders without direction
Then life becomes a path
For meandering fools
A road to nowhere
A meaningless exercise
A pointless excursion
A grand spectacle of futility

But if life is a circle
Then its meaning becomes clear
As we define our journey
And our destiny draws near

Life is a circle
That does not repeat
It drives us with the force of creation
To an ultimate and final destination

The Other

He spent his life fighting those
Who despise the other
Just for being different
Who divide the world into us and them
A lump of coal or a precious gem

He fought to prove the simple truth
We are all human and therefore
Entitled to the same human rights

As I reflect on his life
I know inside he got it right
But I wonder if he fought in vain
For every time we move forward
It seems we move right back again

I'm learning now what he knew then
It's the fight that matters
Not the end

(in memory of my father)

The Irish

The luck of the Irish is in their smile
From the O'Donnell's to the McGarrigle's
From jolly Dublin to County Cork
From Dungan's Hill to Farsetmore

They joined the Brits to fight their wars
And joined the Scotts to fight some more
From the potato famine to Nolan's trial
They fall hard but come back with a smile

The charm of the Irish is in their song
It never matters who's right or wrong
They tap their toes and dance a twirl
From smiling elders to sweet young girls

An ancient people from a rocky land
The Irish have always made a stand
And after every hard-fought battle
They gather together to tip a hand

For the Irish are a resilient set
They stake it all when they place a bet
They've got grit and they've got guile
And when it counts they always smile

They take a hit and come back strong
They clear their throats and sing along
Through every storm and every gale
The Irish spirit will prevail

The Light

In the spring of my youth
I was drawn to the darkness

I gazed at the sea
And saw endless waves of sorrow
I sat the hour of sunset
And contemplated death and destruction
I listened to the caw of the crow
And heard omens of forbearance

In the winter of my old age
I am drawn to light

I gaze at the sea
And see endless waves of promise
I sit the hour of sunset
And feel a renewal of faith
I hear the caw of the crow
And accept its blessing

There is such sweet irony in this
That the closer we move to death
The greater our sense of bliss

The Burden

She carries her burden like water
It glides across her back
Falling gently to the ground
Not allowed to bring her down

She does more for others
Than she has ever done for herself
She gives kindness to strangers
Like candy to kids at Halloween

Down to her last morsel of food
She'll give you half if you ask
She feels sorrow deeper than most
While she wears a contented mask

She gives all she has to kids
No matter what the cost
She would hunt till the stars fall
To find you if you were lost

She cares so much for others
She forgets about herself
She packs away her troubles
And puts them on a shelf

The Sheltered Self

Beneath the shining surface
The part of you that puts on a daily show
There lurks a shaded underbelly
That few will ever know

It is a beast of raw impulses
That Freud designated the Id
It does not harbor the least regret
For the most awful things you did

You keep it sheltered in a cave
Till the moment that you need it
You think that it's your slave
You believe that you can lead it

But when the time of need arrives
The slave becomes the master
And turns your simple life awry
Into a series of disasters

Take a word of sound advice
Keep your monster in its cave
Never let it break the chains
Or let it see the light of day

She Loses Hold

She loses hold of the earth
And swims in her own swirling world
She trusts no one nothing
Not even the ground beneath her feet

She wages battles against the spirits
That hold her tightly in their grasp
Twisting bending wrapping her in their
Spells till she cries out for mercy

She belongs to them for a spell
Before she returns from the netherworld
Of nightmarish fiendish dreams
And wonders where she is
And where she's been

There are times they mark her
They leave a lasting impression
And a certainty they will return
To make their mark again

Down Home in the City

Down home we like our beer light
And our conversations heavy
Down home we grow our men strong
And our lovely women pretty

Ain't never been to New York City

In the town you call the City
We like our beer with bite
We like our women smart and pretty
And we never walk alone

Like you all do down home

Down home we work long hours
We sweat for hard earned wages
Down home we like our steaks rare
And our country songs witty

We don't take to New York City
Down home

In the town we call Manhattan
All the women dress in satin
Our restaurants are the finest
And our wine would make you moan

Like the whiskey down home
In the city

When you get down to the gritty

163

Down home or New York City
We all want the same damn end
To protect our families and friends

Down home in the city

Immortal I

Every man woman and child
From the birth of humankind
From the mother of all creation
To the last of the final calls
At the earth's ultimate fall
Exists now then and always
Beyond memory and time
Beyond the trumpet's last sound
Giving notice to us all

Undeniable ineffaceable
Forevermore
Immortal

Every word and every thought
Every stroll on the beach
Every climb up the mountain
Every talk with an elder
Every hike in the forest
Every footprint in the sand
Every dance and every song
Every feeling we belong
Every gaze at the heavens
Every mission to the stars
Leaves a mark that lasts forever
Declaring who we are

Like the darkness and the spark
Indelible everlasting
Immortal

What is has always been
Will always be…immortal

Go Gently

Dylan Thomas penned the immortal line
Do not go gentle into that goodnight
Rage and fire was his advice
Hold on to that last glimmering glimpse of light

I cannot say if he was wrong or right
He spoke for many who choose to fight
But there are those like me who disagree
Who's preferred last flight is to go gently

When this life ends another begins
I do not wish to spend my final hours
In a fight I cannot win

For me it's a very simple equation:

If I cannot think and cannot write
Let me go gently into that goodnight

The Finale

Have we reached the end?
Toiled to the final tally
Scraped the bottom of the belly?

Are there no more thoughts to think?
Are there no more words of comfort?
Is there nothing more to muse?

No more lessons to absorb
No more scenes of heartlessness or daring
No more disturbing revelations
No more revivals of hope

Song of the nightingale
Stars of the endless sea
An ever-expanding universe
Absorbing the all of me

Have we alas reached the finale?

I sing my song of sorrow
We have reached an end
Goodbye good morrow my friends

The Last Poet

Every generation must wonder
If the last poet has died
With little reason or reflection
We toss the thought aside

In these days of rapid changes
We can no longer be so thoughtless
The poet seems a dying breed
Like the hippo and rhinoceros

But who will sing of tender nights
From dawn to dewy morn
And who will steal a carefree day
When all the world's forlorn

There will always be historians
To make the nation whole
As there must always be poets
To mend the nation's soul

The poet stands beside you
When all else has abandoned
You'll tip a glass and wonder
Is he the last poet standing

(humbly for Jack Foley)

Jazz Baby

A mellow brook gives way
To a stream of flowing water
A flowing stream takes refuge
In a river raging currents swirling
And unseen forces weak and strong
Defiant and unpredictable
Like the moods of midnight love

Take aim at soothing melodies
Knock back the ordinary
The calming and the steady
Cannot satisfy the urge
To Ferlinghetti

Scream in shades of rebel revel
Take an unexpected tour
Find the rhythms unexplored
Like the beast of Mike McClure

Take the highway take the low
Take a bow and stop the show
Settle down and take it easy
Build it back and ask for more
Move it over take the lead
Dare to plant the mortal seed

Can you bring it to its knees
Can you break it make it bleed
Wind it down and make it sooth
Or spin it out and make it daring
Like the sound of metal tearing

Slash your way through the dense jungle
Poison snakes and flying monkeys
Steal a shake from old Slim Shady
Push it fair or pull it foul
Like the cat who made it Howl

Jump a ride on number nine
Let the fumes engulf your brain
When the hazy mist surrounds you
Let him know he's going crazy
Burn it hot and let it singe
Like Bukowski on a binge

Hitch a ride with Wiz to Jazz Town
It's the last stop on the line
Listen long to Ruby singing
Tell her twice that she's sublime
Drink until you're down and dumb
Like the cat in Dharma Bums

The sound of change
Is jazz baby

The time for jazz
Is now

(for Michael McClure et al)

Mother and Child

When the world gave birth to motherhood
The heavens filled with love
When mothers give birth to children
Joy rains down from up above

A child may rage against his mom
A mom may scold her son
But all that anger is forgotten
Before real damage can be done

A mother loves her daughter
More than she loves herself
She will sacrifice her happiness
And place it on a shelf

Oh I've witnessed great emotions
In nature tame or blazing wild
But a stronger love I've never known
Than a mother for her child

(for all the mothers)

Surreality

Woke up to witness an unfamiliar world
Virtual hearings on teleview
Something old trumps something new
Info shaped to point of view
Phones demanding photo time
Virtual hugs on the social line
Surreality blows my mind

I had a dream I can't recall
Poor folks rise and tyrants fall
A joker told me heed the call
Dark clouds fill the western sky
Rain will fall and sun will shine
The reasons do not rhyme
Surreality blows my mind

There are no facts and nothing's true
Up is down and down is through
We operate without a clue
How long before we find
What's yours is sometimes mine
Surreality blows my mind

Space Privateers

I remember when the exploration of space
Was an exalted human endeavor
Not subject to budgetary constraint
But an imperative of the human race

In a battle between dominant nations
The Russians put a man into space
We put a man on the moon
And took the lead in an eternal race

We were once an adventurous people
Who pushed forward against all odds
Now we've sold our lofty ambitions
To the corporate billionaire gods

I once imagined catching a lunar shuttle
To a spaceship bound for Mars
But if it's all about making a profit
We will never reach the stars

Retrospective

In life's progression
We begin in the moment
We take each breath as if it is our last
We have no past nor future
We are at the mercy
Of the encroaching world

There comes a time
We look to an unknown future
We sense its promise
We absorb its mystery
We rush to greet our destiny
As it unmoved slips away

We move from divination
To soulful introspection
We invest countless hours peeling back
Countless layers of masquerade
To discover who we were meant to be

We advance to elder days
And turn our heads around
To view the shadows of our mission
To seal our lessons no longer learning
Writing memoirs and retrospectives
Letting go of passion's yearning

If we are blessed
We reach another stage
Where all of life's enchanted journey
Opens to our introspection

We see the trees beyond the leaves
We view each solitary blade of grass
We begin to understand at last

We end as we began
In the clutches of the moment
More lonely than alone
We have but one more lesson
In the moment we let go

A Poet's Burden

To feel what others dare not feel
To share what others dare not share
To find the pain and suffering
And make a choice to care

To see what others rarely see
To taste a fragrance in the air
To smell the rotting flesh beneath
The naked truth laid bare

If you cut us we will bleed
If you strike us we will fall
Then to lay it down on paper
To be understood by all

To take the knife and thrust it in
To take the blow and rise again
Accept the world for all its sin
It is the poet's burden

For the poet is our conscience
And the poem tells the tale
Without which we would flounder
And our civil order fail

So embrace the humble poet
Hold him to your heart
Let him know that he is valued
For his words and for his art

(humbly for Jack Foley)

Walking in Dreams

In a world of darkness
I seek the light
In a world of wrong
I seek what's right

I walk in dreams of naked beauty
This world does not confine
There are no bars that can contain
The freedom of my mind

I have wept to see the ocean
In all its raging glory
I go there now my love beside
To fulfill a lover's story

I have climbed a mountain
To breathe in a stunning view
And we have stood together
My eyes trained to you

For our lives are entwined
In everything we do
When I walk in my dreams
I walk next to you

Father's Day

I almost forgot Father's Day
Time and thought slipped away
Then a dozen reminders came into view
From all directions in every hue

Who among us does not
Did not have a father?

Mine made an indelible mark
On all his many children
He made us want to change the world
He let us believe we were important
He alone could save us
He alone could make it happen

He seemed surprised when we
Each found our own lives
Our own voices
Our own paths
Through the wilderness

We understood it was our duty
To receive what he handed us
And carry on the legacy

But we went our own way
(just as he did)
Found our own joys
Tasted our own miracles
Breathed our own desires
Discovered our own destinies

As I reach my latter years
I understand
I am more my father
Than I ever understood

Me

I am not my self today
Nor have I ever been
Perhaps I'll find a way to crawl
Into another's skin
And walk amongst the multitudes
Seeing through their eyes
Smelling what they're smelling
Looking at their skies

But I am not my self today
Nor will I ever be
For I have been a sailor
And sailed the open seas
But that was in another life
In truth it was not me

For I am not myself today
I have another soul
I dwell inside a mystery
And live inside a hole
Someday I'll find another
One that I can be
For I am not my self today
And someone is not me

(for the poet Al Green)

The Fountain Pen

Like the feather quill and ink
Like the Underwood word machine
Like the IBM Selectric
The fountain pen is all but extinct
A museum curiosity
A prop for a period play
Extinguished by technology
Cast aside and thrown away

The hours spent committing words
To paper in a most delicate way
A methodology of writing
Poetic prose in an enchanted age

I remember when you could recognize
A poet by the ink stains
On the inside of the middle finger
Or on a once fine shirt
Now tossed in the work bin
When stories always started
Once upon a time
Or once upon a midnight crossing
When poems usually rhymed
And heroes rode white horses
Into silhouetted sunsets

The fountain pen is history
The ball point felt and gel
And soon enough we bid adieu
To paper books and libraries too

Rhythm of the Soul

Detroit
That grinding industrial blues
Chicago
Take the grind and make it smooth
The Delta
Get down to the lowdown blues
N'Orleans
Take the gospel with the Cajun
Memphis
Rock n Soul meets Elvis
Nashville
From country to the hoedown
Austin
Where it all can be found

Every town has its soul
And every soul has its rhythm

Every color and every clime
Rocks to the rhythm of its place and time

Black got a rhythm that's easy to show
White got a rhythm but it rolls slow
Red got a rhythm to a pounding drumbeat
Brown got a rhythm makes you jump to your feet
Yellow got a rhythm lifts the spirit surreal
Green got a rhythm of an earthen feel
Blue got a rhythm of the ocean waves
Blues goes back to the southern slaves

We all got a rhythm deep in our soul

Without it we could never be whole
Find it and don't ever let it go
Cause there's nothing can replace
The rhythm of the soul

The Renaissance Man

The man I always thought to be
A man of learning
A man of creative leaning
A man of letters
A man of art
A man of heart and soul

A man who gathers inspiration
At art museums and music halls
A poet and novelist
A musician and songwriter
A reader of literature
A painter and sculptor
An abstract impressionist
Who finds ecstasy in rainbows
Wonder in children's joy
Harmony in noise

The kind of man you notice
In a world of all the same
A man who walks with pride
While others shrink in shame

The Age of Enlightenment

Have I talked to you about wisdom
The kind that comes with age
The kind that grows to know
Humans at their core
Want to understand
And be understood
Nothing more

Have I talked about desire
The kind that endures
Beneath the surface of beauty
Like the home behind a door
We long for compassion
A bond of caring
Nothing more

Have I spoken of humility
The kind that wisdom embraces
To know perfection in all things
From the beetle to the boar
To love our flaws as our virtues
Nothing less
Nothing more

Old Friends

The ghosts of past adventures
Still haunt the highways and byways
On the road to becoming me
On the path to identity

We left that road so long ago
It no longer exists in this world
We've shaped it with our desires
Polished it with our dreams
Altered it with our memories

Our old friends come to visit
With photos of faded images
That led the long way home
That carved a solemn tome

We share what we can share
Knowing our perceptions
And our experience
Are something short of all
Yet approaching truth
We temper memory
With the kindness of friendship
And agree to tell the story
From the same bridge
The same perch
The same bond of good will

(for Alan Arnopole)

Understanding

A summer wind a midnight still
Are there to be taken in
No thought can round our understanding
We breathe it in and kin

But words and human motivations
Evade our simple senses
Arouse complex emotions
Stimulate our defenses

Every man and woman has an ego
Around which our feelings stir
Do it harm and we will question
Everything we are and were

Strike down the petty little walls
Surrounding our identity
Expose ourselves to sacrifice
And our town becomes a city

We are the center of our being
We cannot be another
But we can open up our view
To engage a sister or brother

A Master of the Word

A mentor
An ancient scribe
A joyful spirit
A man of books and letters
A man of song and dance
A man who gives his knowledge
Freely like the sea
That gives its treasures equally
To all who humbly seek
Oh to see him dance
In his younger days
To see him drink and sing
What pleasure must have
Followed where he led
Greatness did not seek him out
But glory held his hand
And guided him to where
He longed to be
A master of the word
A seeker of secret wisdom
A teller of greater truths
A poet and a teacher
What greater fate could be
What greater destiny

(for Jack Foley on his 80th birthday)

The Shot

Twenty-three and primed for victory
He stepped to the tee on number 16
Zeroed in on his target
Wagged his driver as golfers do
Let loose a mighty swing
Controlled but teeming with power
Eyed it as it climbed through the air
Watched it as it curved sharply
To the waiting flag
Begged it not to turn too much
Let go a sigh as it skirted the trap
And settled eight feet short
Directly on line

It was written in the stars
That this young man
Would bend the flight of the
Ball with his mind
Guide it with his will
At the most opportune time
In the annals of professional golf

At twenty-three
A champion for the ages
A shot for all time
A relief to us all
Who treasure the game
In these tragic and troubled times

We needed this much more
Than this fresh young hero

We needed it to breathe again
We needed it to feel again
That all would one day be normal
And we would not feel guilty
For taking pleasure in simple things
That do not matter

Thank you Collin Morikawa
You will have many more trophies
Many more glorious moments
But none will mean more
To the world than this
Thank you

(Morikawa wins the 2020 PGA Championship)

Gravity

It takes hold of my soul
Presses me down
Like matter in a centrifuge
Water in a pressure cooker
Gas in a confined space
As if the hand of god
Came down upon my forehead
Embracing chest and shoulders
Holding me so still
I cannot think of moving

My body as an ornament
A useless lump of mass
A burden to the spirit
Damned and damaged goods
Discarded by the roadside

I feel its binding grasp
I sense its awesome force
Omnipresent omnipotent
Like the god of stillness
The god of indifference
The god of somnolence
The god of wait steady hold
And wonder why it bothers
And wonder what's foretold

I am here I am gone
I am dreaming
Was I dreaming all along?

Take this weight
And let me fly away
Let me wander let me roam
Release my body
And guide me home

Heat

It comes in waves
If you watch the horizon
You can see it
If you walk the streets at noon
You can feel it rising
You can smell it
If you wait for it
You can taste it

It rides the salty waves
Wraps around your body
Covers you in perspiration
And slowly
Like a caterpillar on a twig
Wears you down

It settles in the pores
Of your hot wet skin
It burrows in
Crawls through vessels
Enters your brain
Medulla oblongata
Cerebellum cerebrum
Pounding
Like the wheels
Of a locomotive train
Pounding
Like the beating heart of fear
Like waves drawing near

It settles in

And steals your free will
Puts your faith on hold
Waiting waiting
For the cover of night
The promise of sweet respite
Awakened by morning light

(Record heat wave CA August 2020)

Damnation

Thinking of things I should have done
Battles lost we should have won
Crooks and thieves we should have caught
But it's too damned hot

Watching the clouds roll slowly by
Counting every tick of the clock
Time to think and time to not
When it's too damned hot

Wished we'd have moved
Wish that a lot
So many things we should have got
But it's too damned hot

Should have played the piano
Should have mastered guitar
Many skills we wish we'd been taught
When it's too damned hot

I'll go down by the river
Cool my feet on the rocks
Lose myself in idle thought
Cause it's too damned hot

(a record 106 in central California
August 16, 2020)

More in Common

I used to hate folks from Texas
They brought ruination and shame
But it wasn't the people of Texas
It was just the political game

Folks are pretty much the same all over
If you take them for granted
If you treat em like dirt
Then they give you nothing but trouble
But if you treat em with respect
Then they give it back to you
Sometimes double

So when it comes to the truth
It's more than plain to see
Those folks ain't much different
Than you and me

Folks are pretty much the same
No matter where you abide
We have a lot more in common
Than we have that divides

Rest in Peace

When one we admire
Or one we love
Falls from this earthly realm
It is with compassion and love
We respond
Rest in peace

One wonders in reflection
If that is what the fallen desires
When an individual has spent a lifetime
Fighting for justice
Fighting for peace
Fighting against the fist of oppression
Is it eternal peace one desires

When I travel to the world beyond
(as I choose to believe there is such a place)
I do not wish to spend forever in peace
I do not wish to rest in perpetuity

Rest in peace may do for others
Not for me
I wish to be challenged
I desire to move forward
I strive to rise above

Therefore when I rise or fall
From this mortal existence
Let those who love me
Or hold me in esteem
Not wish that I should rest in peace

But that I should gather the strength
In death that I had in the prime of life
To continue the fight

For there will always be darkness
And there will always be light
Let me stand my ground
With the good and the right

The Burden

The young carry the burden
The old must leave behind
What greater burden could be left
Than the one that we now find

A generation of negligence
We're the ones who forgot the world
We sought out our own adventures
While the earth's demise unfurled

We didn't mean for it to happen
We just forgot to ask
About our role as caretakers
We neglected our basic task

You have a right to be angry
We handed you this mess
We can say we didn't know
We're not guilty we protest

We were seeking higher consciousness
And for some it may be true
But we failed to hold the horror back
Failed to push change through

Young Man

Young man young man
Oh where will you go
What future do you see
What seeds will you sow
This world is inside out
You'd have to be a fool
If you weren't filled with doubt
Everything you see and touch
Everything you feel and know
Scattered like the dust
The way the wind blows
We have taken your world
Flipped it on its head
Due to our neglect
Millions are dead
Does it matter that we're sorry
Does it matter we regret
We are like the lost horizon
Won't be here to pay the debt
But you hold the dream
And you are the hope
Young man young man
Oh where will you go

Young Woman

Young woman young woman
What path will you take
Will you bury the past
This world to forsake
Will you forgive all those
Who shook the earth to its core
Will you seek a new start
Will you open a door
Will you burn the bridge behind you
Will you bid us farewell
When you have your own children
What stories will you tell
About those who came before you
Who forgot the ones to come
Who were blind to the future
To the past deaf and dumb
What love will you harbor
What hearts will you break
Young woman young woman
What path will you take

Old Man

Old man old man
What can you do
You have lived your life
You must now say adieu
Will you retreat inside
Will you push the world away
Will you plead for one last ride
One last plan to go astray
You had so many chances
To change what went wrong
But you were lost in your world
You were tossed in your song
Now you've made your bed and garden
It's too late to change the end
You look back on your deeds
And the wreck you must defend
They will turn the world over
They will make the earth anew
Old man old man
What can you do

Old Woman

Old woman old woman
Will you look back on the years
Will you reside in yesterday
Will you dry your tears
Will you search lost memories
For better times and better ways
Leave your worries behind
Let your problems fade
Will you find the lord above
Will you move on or stay
Where you're most loved
Where you're most safe
Will you stop and take stock
Of all the things you did not say
All the stories left untold
All the debts you did not pay
When you got old and it got late
The morning light turned to gray
And you accepted life's cruel fate
The last act closes the curtain falls
The end of all draws near
Old woman old woman
Will you look back with tears

Little Boy

Little boy little boy
What will you be
Will you work in the fields
Will you sail on the sea
Will you run for high office
Will you march on the streets
Will you conquer an army
Will you manage defeat
Will you take what you're given
Will you settle for less
Will you value the truth
Will your deeds be blessed
Will you still find joy
In moments of glee
Little boy little boy
What will you be

(for Grayson & Logan)

Little Girl

Little girl little girl
What dreams will you dream
Will you dance in the heavens
Will you play on the team
Will you find true love
To help you along
Will you always be willing
To sing your own song
Have you set your sights
On a future of gold
Will you climb a tall mountain
Before you get old
Will you find that life
Is not quite what it seemed
Little girl little girl
What dreams will you dream

(for Lilliana, Ellie, and Addie)

Ghost Woman

Ghost woman ghost woman
Why do you linger
I taste your damp breath
I feel your cold finger
Your love is so strong
You cannot let it go
Your sorrow runs deep
And your tears still flow
You have gone to your grave
With love in your heart
Care is your legacy
Compassion your art
You have given to others
The best of your soul
Now the time has come
For your spirit to go
Hear the sweet voice
And the follow the singer
Ghost woman ghost woman
No more will you linger

Dead Man

Dead man dead man
Where have you gone
Have you met your sweet maker
Have you known all along
Are you walking with angels
Does your spirit now soar
Have you answered the question
What was it all for
Do you ever look back
On those you still love
As they pray to heaven
Do you pray from above
Do you miss our presence
As we surely miss yours
Will you wait for us kindly
As we pass through the door
Does a new world await
Like a bright new dawn
Dead man dead man
Where have you gone

No Harm

Mama taught me a lot of lessons
And most of them were true
Before you leave the house
Make sure you tie your shoes
Don't be afraid to say you're sorry
If you find you're in the wrong
Always speak up for the weak
Always know where you belong
If you're in a crowded theater
Do not sound the alarm
If you can't do something helpful
Do no harm
Do no harm

If you fall get right back up
If you fail try again
You can't win every battle
But you can rise in the end
Don't fall for smooth talkers
Don't believe in fool's charm
If you can't do something useful
Do no harm
Do no harm

Dark Shadows

They crawl out of the cracks
Of America's nightmare
Loom in the hazy background
Watching with great care
Ready to pounce
Spinning a lair
Taking a life
On a dare

They mark the path of a fools parade
Following those who do not know
Who did not care
Go with the flow
A defiant stare
All for the show
Too much to bear

They carry a seed of deadly disease
It steals your breath away
Makes you weak and feeble
Makes your body sway
It has the number
You must pay
The shadow knows
The shadow grows
So bow your head
And pray

Bravado

We are all subject to the laws of physics
We cannot opt out
We cannot object on moral grounds
The sun will rise
The moon will follow
Young folks reach for the sky
Old folks like fallen fruit must die
Don't ask why
Don't ask why

You can curse the stars for shining
You can purge what rests within
You can dwell in sorrow's garden
You can argue with the wind

A single truth survives the ages
Upon this you can depend
The greatest lesson in this life
Comes at its very end

It's the moment when you realize
A mere flash before the fall
Your courage in the face of death
Wasn't bravery at all

Desperate Hours

Woke up with a song by John Prine
Running like a stray dog
Through the alleys of my mind
Started thinking about the Desperate Hours
That old noir with Bogart and March
When everything was black and white
When heroes were always golden boys
And always got their man
When villains were evil head to foot
And always got what they deserved
Bogie was different
His villains had character
Like Dobbs in Sierra Madre
Badges? We don't need no stinking badges!
His heroes were flawed
Like Richard Blane in Casa Blanca
You played it for her
You can play for me
If she can take it I can
Play it Sam
…
Funny thing
I can't remember how the movie ends
Ain't that a kick in the cerebellum
…
That's the way the world go round
It makes you smile it makes you frown
It picks you up and it puts you down
That's the way the world…goes round

211

Return to Kind

Somewhere on the blue highways
Of my mind
I remember hearing this fertile valley
Was once a barren desert

All things return to kind
What once was will be again
The dam will give way
The river will run its course
The forest will reclaim the cities
The irrigated desert will return to sand
And we poor humans will return
Kicking and screaming like banshees
On a moonlit night
To our more natural lives

Our towers will topple
Civilizations decline
Earth will reclaim her majesty
In the richness of time

The Lotus

The beauty of the lotus flower
Lifts our spirits in the darkest hour
Calms our frayed and fragile nerves
Makes the burden of our mind less

In times of tragedy and death
Our minds will seek levity and jest
To lift us from our jaded view
That bears no joy or kindness

We turn back to the lotus
As it finds a way to float us
On the deep deep pool of sorrow
To which time and trouble bind us

There is beauty in the world as yet
And if we ever should forget
Just take another look around
The lotus will remind us

The Sacred Crow

I gazed into the eyes of the crow
And saw what came to be
Days of darkness nights of fear
Catastrophe in threes

We tasted fruit from the poison tree
Where many fell and did not rise
The crow will always find its way
Piercing a sea of lies

I saw a scarred and barren land
From the eyes of the crow in flight
Trees ripped from their mother's womb
A horrid tortured sight

I saw the land turn dry and crack
Cities swallowed by the sea
Smoke filled skies and burnt horizons
No place of rest to comfort me

The crow escapes to untouched heights
And leaves me far behind
To seek what solace welcomes me
What fate for me unwinds

If we measure pure intelligence
By the talent to survive
The human will long vanish
The sacred crow will thrive

Be more like the crow

That lives within its means
That leaves the land intact
And honors what it dreams

Honor

It is a privilege to be selected
Quite the opposite to be neglected
What to the chosen is an honor
Is like an invite to the party Donner

So while I don't wish to be a critic
I must turn off my analytic
That smooths this square to round
It falls to me on shaky ground

I don't believe in competition
Where art is on the stage
What seems a lesser work today
Like wine improves with age

We should not write for accolades
We should not aim to please
The desperate need for recognition
Becomes a grim disease

So in the end I must decline
An honor not bestowed
I'll keep my honor to myself
At peace in my abode

The Gateway

They stormed the gates of the Bastille
They stormed the gates of Brandenburg
They stormed the gates at Buchenwald
They stormed the gates of hell

Whenever change is needed
Wherever people are bound
Whatever hand oppresses
A gateway must be found

We are known for building barriers
We are famed for building walls
But a wall without a gateway
Is a wall that must soon fall

A way to bend both time and space
A gateway to beyond
A path to save the human race
And build a stronger bond

We are trapped within an endless maze
Desperate to escape
We are searching for a gateway
To take a leap of faith

Purgatory

There is a place on earth
Between heaven and hell
Where the land is on fire
Where the senses rebel
Where the air smells of smoke
Where the leader laughs
And calls it a joke

There is a place on earth
Where the frozen tundra melts away
Where caution runs and folly stays
Where homes burn to the ground
And the land runs dry
Where grown men break down
And strong women cry

This is a land of prophecy
A dying breed
Where one world ends
And another takes seed

The Bitter End

In this long life I've seen it all
Monsters rise and virtues fall
On this sad fate you can depend
We're heading for a bitter end

The endless hours are unrestrained
The human race has gone insane
There are no crimes we can't defend
Welcome to the bitter end

We hear preachers spinning riddles
Accompanied by fiddles
Screaming in the hollow nights
No relief within our sight
Sorrow's message they do send
Welcome to the bitter end

We see four horsemen on the rise
Terror burns in desperate eyes
They have no helping hand to lend
Welcome to the bitter end

We stand strong and defiant
We will become self-reliant
Will not break though we may bend
Though we meet the bitter end

Survive

A rolling spectacle of misery
The loneliness of isolation
The scourge of homelessness
The prospect of destitution
The hopelessness of prostitution
The stain of human bondage
The glorification of violence
The deification of criminality
The universality of suffering
A failing will to stay alive
Yet do not worry little ones
We have not lost our drive
We will survive

The western world on fire
A raging mother earth
Prophecies most dire
Pray for what it's worth
The sound of towers crashing
The cry of souls in pain
Slaves receive a lashing
Tears like pounding rain
Yet do not worry little ones
Though hard times have arrived
Be strong and keep your head
We will survive

The Light

Pray for forgiveness
Pray for second sight
End this madness
Follow the light

For we have lived too long
Suffered too many lies
Cried too many tears
Sacrificed too many lives
To hang our weary heads now
And give up the good fight
Find your courage and
Follow the light

For I have witnessed darkness
And I have seen its face
It always pretends to care
As it fills our empty space
But we reject their message
As we stand up for the right
Stern your resolve
Follow the light

For we have dwelled so long
In the caverns of darkness
Even the thought of light
Delivers palpitations of the heart
Our eyes close in fright
As if thought alone
Could damage our sight
Discard all distraction and

Follow the light

For we have breathed this toxic air
So long we think it's healthy
When others have nothing
Having something seems wealthy
And we have sought our comfort
In shared grief and mourning
So long it sings us goodnight
Stand up stand strong
Reach out for the light

Come now the light will guide you
Into our mother's loving arms
And it will make you whole again
And it will make you strong
Let it raise you to its lofty height
Find your strength inside
Come home to the light

Honest

Never trust a banker
A banker is a wanker
Never trust a broker
A broker is a joker

Real estate is not real
Property is not proper
The products of imagination
Given to pure speculation

A nation is not a nation
That does not know how to share
And does not care

Never trust a man woman
Or child who says:
Trust me

(Trust me not)

Anyone who postulates
If I'm being honest
Is caught.

Honest
       Fair
              Candid
Real

Trust your gut
How it makes you feel

Fire Wind & Rain

The horsemen ride
The end is nigh
A land of ruins
A fire sky

By fire wind and rain
By gales on wings of thunder
By flood and raging flames
The world we tossed asunder

We call forth all our fears
A quaking of the earth
Mother Mary holds us near
The end calls forth the birth

The planet now has fallen
Under a deep and dark spell
Sound a thousand alarums
Ring the solemn bell

Dark clouds of mortal ruin
Have descended upon us
Our drinking water is poisoned
Our sky has become jaundiced

We need fundamental change
Something or someone to save us
No more lying boasting politicians
Who only want to enslave us

Find your Bliss

When days are dark and hazy
When waking is a chore
When at your best you're lazy
When every nerve is bored
Take stock of all you know
And just remember this:
Find your bliss

The death toll keeps on ringing
The impulse is to weep
The sirens keep on singing
Our leaders went to sleep
Do not become forlorn
Think of what you'd miss
Find your bliss

Every cloud a silver lining
Every fall a rise above
Cease the never-ending whining
Greet worry with a shove
Start the day with a kiss
And remember this:
Find your bliss

(In memory of Joseph Campbell)

Words Flow

Words flow
Like the wind blows
In a tropical storm
On a raging sea

What can it be?
What can it be?

Thoughts course
Like the river goes
Through a granite canyon
On a millennial run

It has begun
It has begun

Emotions follow
Like a child's growth
In the teenage years
When the heart explodes

Where does it go?
Where does it go?

Dreams float
Like the sky snows
In Sierra winters
On an open road

What does it show?
What does it show?

My mind opens
Like a clear blue sky
When a drifting cloud
Comes floating by

Don't know why
Don't know why

Vengeance II

The path of vengeance
Is not easily taken
But when the nation
To its core is shaken
We must act in accord
With conscience

There is a line
We dare not cross
Lest we sacrifice ourselves
In our souls we sense the loss
Our compass on a shelf

Our enemies are great and strong
And morally bereft
They pull us where we don't belong
We fear there's nothing left

There will be no vengeance taken
Not today nor tomorrow
We will suffer through the madness
And exorcise our sorrow

Tomorrow will be better
Better still the day after
For we will find the key to hope
In faith and in laughter

Pride

Proudly down the street she walks
Not a care in sight
What a joy it is to know
You're absolutely right

There is no hesitation
As she strolls along the street
She casts a knowing eye
At everyone she meets

To walk with such great certainty
One wonders will she falter
And if she does one wonders
Will her path be altered

For though pride we must harbor
We need temper it with doubt
Best to keep our faith inside
Than to bandy it about

Small Betrayals

Woke with scattered memories
Of betrayals large and small
Made me wonder if my friends
Are not my friends at all

Took a moment then recalled
We are only momentary imprints
On a vast and changing sea
Friendship is the greatest gift
That anyone can bring

Those large betrayals weren't so large
The small ones were so small
Let them be and let them go
For every grudge must fall

Why hang on to the burdens
That belong to yesterday
Just stack them up before you
And blow them all away

The Longest Hours

From the hours of the deepest night
To the hours of early morn
When sleep no longer comforts
My thoughts become forlorn

I wonder if we cannot do
What destiny demands of us
I wonder if we cannot see
What history commands of us

Are you and I accountable
For this collapse of reason
Our failings to this point in time
May fall just short of treason

In the hours of the deepest night
To the hours of early morn
My musings chase the darkness
My nightmares are reborn

Golden Years II

Whatever happened to the golden years
That gentle time of life
When all the hardships slip away
When grandma and grandpa
Spend carefree days
With frolicking kids at play

When time though precious is free
When all the bills are paid
And we retire to the calming sea
When no more plans are laid
We're allowed to simply be
Until we are no longer capable
Of our basic daily chores
Like cooking lunch and dinner
Or going to the store

Whatever happened to those years
They belong to yesterday
Now we have a flood of worries
A runaway virus hospital stays
And too many bills to pay

Gone

The mist of a Pacific storm
The fog of a redwood forest
The scent of blooming passion
The wisp of a loved one's sigh

Capture the moments you treasure
Seize them by the core
Breathe them in and never let go
Store them where they're safe and warm
Let them comfort and ease your soul

Gone now are the late night runs
Gone the endless nights till dawn
Gone are the moonlight drives
Gone the way of carefree lives

We look back now with yearning
The inner fire no longer burning
Wondering where the passion went
The lifeblood of longing spent

We live our lives never knowing
Our true feelings never showing
Here today and gone tomorrow
Holding back our love and sorrow

When we spend more time
With what has been
Than we do with what will be
We'll know that life
In all its humbling mystery
Has passed us by

Perspective

The world has taken a horrid turn
If there's anything left
There's something to learn
We've gone our own ways
No thought for our brothers
A tilt of the axis
And we'll lose all the others

We've taken a ride
On a suicide train
Can't stay dry when
You're nude in the rain
Moving faster and faster
When we should slow down
Crops don't grow on
Dry cracked ground

There's got to be a better way
Don't we all know it?
You feel it in your heart
But you're afraid to show it

Take a long look around
Don't like what you see?
Change your perspective
See what it could be

There are many other ways
All better than this
But it will not get better
Without cease and desist

A Man with Two Hearts

A man with two faces
Has learned to deceive
A man with two tongues
Cannot be believed
A man of two minds
Remains paralyzed
A man with two hearts
Can never be wise
For his affection follows
His wandering eyes
He cannot be trusted
Nor should be despised
For his love is shallow
With no lasting ties
His fate is sorrow
Be it fall or rise

The Soul

Have I spoken to you of the soul?
Have I spoken of the center of life?
Have I spoken to you about that
Which remains when all else fades?
Have I spoken to you of the soul?

In the spring of life
When the body blooms
And draws to earthly pleasures
Like wildlife to a fertile garden
When desire is everything
And heartbreak takes its toll
There is no need of soul

In the summer of youth
When the mind opens to a world
Of endless possibilities
We step out of our safe confines
To explore the open road
In search of adventure and awe
Seeking secrets of our yearning
We wonder what it's like to grow old
We discover the hidden soul

In the autumn of our journey
We seek the knowledge of elders
And the wisdom of vision seekers
Our thoughts turn to darkness
We become aware of Death
That powerful and mystic friend
We don't want our lives to end

Before we learn and know
The contents of our soul

In the winter of our descent
We seek calm and peace of mind
We seek to pass our knowledge on
To those in love we hold
We have reached our lifelong goal
We have uncovered our soul

Have I spoken to you of the soul?
Have you found your place in life?
Have you located the meaning
That makes your life whole?
Have you asked what I've learned?
Would you like to know?
Have we talked about the soul?

For What it's Worth

The taste of fresh clean water
A sparkling stream
A moonlit sky
A drive along the coast highway
Hearing Santana for the first time
Jazz on the Coltrane
A walk in Central Park
Laughter in a canyon
The smile of a stranger
A strong steady girth
The things we take for granted
For what it's worth

A fine wine at dinner
Rest at the end of a ride
Visions of an eagle's flight
A dance of muses
Botticelli's masterworks
A magic bus to the heavens
A dive to ocean depths
The crisp high mountain air
Kids on a playground
The miracle of birth
The things we take for granted
For what it's worth

Tracking down a long fly ball
A kite on the wind
The scent of cinnamon pastry
The immortal soul of Billie Holiday
A floating white cloud

The mourning cry of a dying sun
The song of a rising moon
The glory of Crazy Horse
A warm fire on a frigid night
Life on planet earth
The things we take for granted
For what it's worth

Sleep

The miracles of science astound
A medicine for every ailment
A pill for every problem
Yet nature has its own solutions
Organic cures and common sense
Grandma's balms and ointments
Herbs and spices handed down
Across the generations

The greatest medicine of all is sleep
Sweet natural nocturnal sleep
The gentle journey into dream
The dive into the great unknown
The land of liquid mountains
Rolling terrains of land and sea
Where the spirit is renewed
Where the soul is liberated
From its earthly shackles

To sleep and be reborn
In health and perfect balance
The miracle of sleep

A Symphony in Stone

A thousand ancient circles of stone
Tributes to antiquity
Placed with secret knowledge
Balance and perfect harmony

Carved and shaped with care
In accord with sacred formulae
Aligned with stars and planets
A pleasure to the heart and eye

Gothic castles and cathedrals
Messages to the gods
Humble pleas for understanding
Of divine and natural laws

Behold a mythic glimpse of light
A symphony in stone
And know in all the universe
Humanity is not alone

The Commons

They used to be our parents
Before they became our grandparents
Now they live a world away
At the Commons

They listen to the gentle wind
They used to be rockers
They used to drive Cadillacs
Now they drive walkers
They've learned to love simple things
At the Commons

They don't ask for a lot
A weekly visit a decent meal
They desire things that comfort
For the things that make them feel
In the company of friends
At the Commons

This world once belonged to them
Now they are dependent
They keep their thoughts to themselves
Until wisdom is ascendent
At the Commons

Take a close look around
Give them kindness and respect
For we are but a breath away
From becoming introspect
At the Commons

Papa be Proud

My father left this mortal earth
Too soon it seems to me
We never had a chance to share
Our inmost thoughts and dreams

When he was here I wondered
Though I never spoke aloud
Papa, when you think of me
Are you happy? Are you proud?

For I lived my life in shadows
Doing what I was allowed
Until I found my calling
And took a solemn vow

I sang my song in public
Sang it strong and sang it loud
I cried out for justice
Before an angry crowd
I always dreamed of rising
Above the highest cloud
Now I look back and wonder
Papa, are you proud?

Mates

We have been together long enough to know
We have always been so
We understand each other
We complement each other
We have learned to accept our eccentricities
We have learned to temper our tempers
With love and compassion
We know each other
Our hearts and our souls
We believe in each other
We know that love only grows
To end of days
Love only grows

Kansas

Kansas is autumn
Kansas is gently falling leaves
Kansas is a whispering wind
Kansas is a moment of peace
On a whirlwind crazy day
California is where you're headed
Kansas is where you stayed

Missouri Kansas Oklahoma
Tornado alley home sweet home
Uncle Henry Auntie Em
Dorothy and Toto too
The windswept plains
Fields of Plenty
Grapes of Wrath
A place of yesterday
Tennessee is where you came from
Kansas is where you stayed

A Social Conscience

Fundamental to life
All beings possess a social conscience
Crows guard collective territory
Wolves howl to warn the pack
Whales sing empathic sorrow
Dolphins swarm to protect the weak

When we speak we speak in all voices
When we sing we add to the symphony
Of all humanity throughout time

The triumph of one inspires all
The tragedy of one breaks all hearts

We are born without greed
We are born without selfishness
We are born to be socially aware
We are born to serve and care
We are born to rise above ourselves
To seek the comfort of our fellow beings

Greed is a disease of the soul
Humility is the cure

Pity those who are wrapped within themselves
Who cannot see beyond their own reflection
For they are warped and tortured beings
Destined to grief and loneliness

The Long Road

When the needs of now are pressing
The needs of tomorrow cease
Like coins in a piggy bank
For payments on a lease

We cannot see the horizon
For the haze within our eyes
For the fear rising within our hearts
For the poison in our skies

The karmic debt is mounting
While we poor souls are still
Counting and recounting
Coins to pay the bill

We are stranded by the roadside
In a far off lonely place
On a road that leads to nowhere
Staring blankly into space

The way ahead is long and hard
We know it in our bones
But the only choice we have is
To go together or alone

For mother earth will take her toll
She will not be ignored
All living things are equal
All people rich and poor

The Window

To the window must I go
To have a visit with my soul
Wondering where my vision went
Beyond the past my time is spent

I'll dig no further through the pages
That tell me where I've been
A burning fire through me rages
Against the reign of men

I turn my back on all I've seen
All I've said and all I've done
All I've learned is little more
Than the little world of one

To the window I must go
Where I've never gone before
To seek a vision of the future
To the past I close the door

An open window is the key
To everything I wish to see
Beyond the view of mortal eyes
I will wear no more disguise

When at last I understand
The truth beyond our view
I'll return to take a stand
And share my truth with you

The Vision

Through the lens of his vision
He saw what others could not see
He plugged into a hidden mind
That lives inside of you and me

He tore away the old framework
And created something new
The spirit of inventiveness
That lives inside of me and you

He observed the machination
Examined part by part
Rewired and reconfigured
Transplanted its very heart

We are not what we are
It is not what it is or seems
The stone is not a stone
We live inside of dreams

For one must see without one's eyes
Feel without one's senses
You then begin to understand
How small the picket fence is

(for Rich Curtis)

A New Day

It looms ever ahead
Advancing and receding
Like a mirage on a lonesome highway

We reach for it
Touch it taste it consume it
And it is gone
Gone
Forever always gone
And we poor souls
Are left lonely and afraid
Longing for yesterday's dream

A new day dawns
Nature erupts in song
Spirits dance on treetops
The small and bountiful belong

We are born to new purpose
And we are on the path
We will plead for forgiveness
Make amends for nature's wrath

Every particle is filled
With hope and good will
You can sense it deep within
If you sit long and still

It's a new day
There's a new way
Rejoice and sing

Letting Go

A creeping madness found its way
Into the national psyche
It clouded our vision with venom

The long shadows of these days remain
Like the taste of meat gone bad
Lingering and taking its toll
On every living thing it touches

It makes us grow old
Before our time

We want to sit for a hundred years
And contemplate the meaning
But we cannot
The urgency of the moment
Propels us forward
We cannot sleep
We cannot eat
We dare not drink
We can hardly breathe

We want to let it go
But the madness will not
Let go of us

Spirits of Halloween

Tonight the spirits dance
In the forest of eternal darkness
Tonight the dead gain voice
Wolves howl at a screaming full moon
Monsters hide in cracks and shadows
Demons rise from the bowels of earth
Evil trumps innocence
Spiders and crawly things swarm
Our towns and cities
Awakening the beating heart of fear
Vampires and zombies
Werewolves and swamp creatures
Witches and warlocks
Take hold of the human psyche
Grasp it with their slimy fingers
And squeeze

Tonight the spirits of Halloween dance
And we lost souls dance with them

The Dream

Understanding across humanity
Empathy for the poor
An end to hunger and starvation
Poverty no more

Equality across the races
Decent homes for everyone
Jobs at living wages
We must work until it's done

No more wars in other nations
To boost the corporate treasure
No more punishing the powerless
To serve our morbid pleasure

We will build it from the ground up
A tribute to all that's good
Not a monument to the past
But to show we understood

The dream is not over
It has only just begun
When all the votes are counted
The people will have won

Last Man Standing *

So many battles in my days
Of wandering on my own
Looking for the answers
When the questions are unknown

I have seen both sides of love
I have won and I have lost
For every battle win or lose
We all pay a heavy cost

I have seen my loved ones fall
And I have known the glory
I have suffered through it all
To tell a lonesome story

For I have climbed the mountain
And here I stand alone
Gazing down at what has been
Trying to atone

There is no answer in my view
Or none that I can see
We live our separate lives
And accept what is will be

(* Bruce Springsteen's latest album)

Faith

A legacy of lies and broken promises
To believe and be betrayed
To place one's heart in another's hands
To feel it as it breaks

Trust is a treasured possession
We invest it in our friends
When returned in rank deception
Friendship surely ends

We have lost our faith in others
We have lost our sense of one
Abandoned sisters and brothers
The days of belonging done

We must find our way back home
To a place of love and caring
Where the spirit of giving prospers
Where prosperity breeds sharing

The Town and the City

When you live in the city
They beat you down
Til you come around
Til you get along
Til you sing their song
In harmony

When you live in a town
They beat you up
Til you drink from the cup
Til you breathe the air
Til you take the dare
And you only care
For the humble fare

If you want to understand
Your fellow woman or man
You must spend some time
Hearing others rhyme
Go inside their minds
Drink their wine
And go back home
To ponder

When those from the town
Have spent time in the city
And those in the city
Have spent time in the town
We will all understand
Five fingers to a hand
Commonalities of man

And woman

Those who never venture never see
The isolate can never be free
Until he comes of age
Learns to break the cage
Of homespun dogma
And prejudice

Untethered

We have wandered so far from the ropes
We no longer know where we started
Where we end is beyond the scope
We are untethered unbound adrift
Floating aimlessly on an open sea

We have forgotten why we began
This endless journey to unknown lands
Each day we awaken to a new dream
Reality has strayed from our grasp
We reach for it and it slinks away
We dive for it as it turns to dust
We conjure it in distant memories

We have become separate and aloof
While our concrete world escapes
We claim the right to invent the
Planets and the stars that reign over
Our waking lives in day and night
Even our dreams are borrowed

We were not born this way
The real world once fed and nurtured us
We grew and prospered in its grace
We suffered in stubborn defiance

When and how did we lose touch
How and when did we lose hold
When did life slip from our senses
Who cut the ties that bound us
To this breathing pulsing earth

We must find our way home
We must plant our feet on solid ground
We must feel the wind and taste the air
We must learn to love our lives again
We must love our gracious mother
In all her teeming splendor

Masters

Masters of war
KEEP THE PEACE
Masters of diplomacy
FIGHT BACK WAR
Masters of politics
PROTECT DEMOCRACY
Masters of art and music
ENRICH OUR DAILY LIVES
Masters of the written word
GIVE US MEANING
Masters of the game
GIVE US JOY
Masters of crime
ENGAGE OUR MINDS
Masters of detection
HOLD CRIME IN LINE
Masters of medicine
KEEP US WELL
Masters of the human psyche
KEEP US BALANCED

To be a master
Is to attain the highest level
Of knowledge and achievement
In a given field

The world needs masters
More than ever
But more than that
The world needs to believe
In them

John Brown

Slavery is an abomination
A crime against the soul
A stain upon the holy word
A pestilence on humankind
Civilization in decline

Praise be glory to god
The righteous shall prevail
The children of evil will fall
And posterity will sing glory
Praise and glory to all

We do not fear death
For our cause is god's cause
And we shall rise to his embrace
And he shall know us by our dignity
And he shall know us by our grace
For we are god's servants
On this lonely planet earth
And he shall take us in his loving arms
For he shall recognize our worth
Now and forever
Amen

It was a glorious victory
Everybody died

Space X

The great mystery remains
The exploration of space
No greater mission of discovery is
Destined for the human race

We have tapped beyond the sun's reach
We have grasped the surface of Mars
We have bent the force of gravity
We have peeked beyond the stars

What greater purpose can there be
Than to explore the mysteries of space
To test the depths of understanding
To recognize our place

We must always expand our thinking
Set aside our little lives
There is so much to see and know
The goals for which we strive

We are better than we have been
We must see beyond our worth
We will see it all with new eyes
No longer tethered to the earth

Blame the Moon

When people you know
Become people you don't
When your heart demands action
But somehow you won't
When your life turns backwards
And your insides turn out
When you want to move on
But you're paralyzed by doubt
When you want to protest
But you fear it's too soon
Blame it on the moon
Like they used to do
Blame it on the moon
When you haven't a clue

In the distant past superstition ruled
Wisdom delivered by priests and fools
Everyone walked the same old walk
Everyone talked the same old talk
Everyone dreamed the same dream
And danced to the same old tune
When something went wrong
They sang a new song and
Blamed it on the moon

So it could be now
Or it could be the past
Some things die out
While other things last

We often look to what came before

To understand our reality
When tragedy comes from a distant shore
We blame it on the angry sea
We blame it on the loons
Or blame it on the lovely moon
Just don't blame it on me

Finding Gratitude

If there is no hunger where you live
Be grateful to the earth that gives
If you're not exposed to a wind that roams
Be grateful for your sturdy home
If you have friends and ones you love
Be grateful to the stars above
If you have found one pure of heart
Give thanks you'll never be apart
If you smile and laugh in ample measure
Be thankful for the simple pleasure
If you have a warm family circle
Be grateful for the ties that bind
If you're blessed with common courtesy
Be grateful for a world that's kind

No matter what and where we are
We can always be grateful
We should thank our lucky stars
We have not become hateful

For there is love in all things
And there are those who care
And the one above does not give us
Troubles we can't bear

Hard times tell us what really matters
Lesser things will fall and scatter

Iliad

He sings of endless sorrow
He sings of eternal war
An ancient never-ending war
A war for the amusement of gods

A stolen beauty
A burning grudge
A summoning of the dead
But not forgotten
Never forgotten
Not as long as good people remember
Not as long as the story is told
By lonely poets and hungry storytellers

A story of war across millennia
A story of vengeance and pride
A lament of the dead and dying
Spirits still living in the stench-filled air
Spirits without voices or words
Only tears flowing like rivers of sorrow

The pride of Agamemnon
The cowardice of Paris
The affection of Aphrodite
The courage of Hector
The blood of the masses
The fall of Achilles
The indifference of kings
Honor dishonored in war

Nine years of war

The normalization of death
The rage of the gods abated
Only the dead remain

All is destiny
The gods have no mercy
The goddesses no love
All is mourning and loss

Performance

Well done! Bravo!
A virtuoso performance!

He lives for this
To attract all eyes
To feel the admiration of strangers
The applause
The rising uplift of clapping hands
A voice reaching for the stars
A spirit rising
Giving all

To give so much for others
To sacrifice oneself
To live and die for the stage
For the play
For the eternal moment
When all hearts break
When emotions emerge
And roar into the open air

To speak the voice of the gods
To feel the power
If only for a fleeting moment

I came
I stood
I made my mark
And now it is done
I bow

(applause)

Bravo! Well done!

Book of Forms

Because it was written long ago
Some will say it must be so
Perhaps it was written that god embraces
A privileged class of superior races
Some would say it must be so
Why? It is written
And so some are smitten
With antiquities
Not I

I must find my own forms
My own guiding principles
My own codes and philosophies
Let others walk the trodden path
I will brave the unspoiled forest
Of dreams and novel mythologies
Knowing that many years from now
My path may also be trodden
And braver souls will find
A braver and bolder way
To keep the faith

Inward Gaze

(Song of Self)

Days dark we develop our inward sight
Days bright we look outward to joyful light
We should always savor our better days
For soon they are buried in bitter haze

The days have grown colder the night so long
We doubt our feelings and sing a sad song
We walk through the woods on a misty day
Wandering we fear we will lose our way

At times I lose myself inside myself
And then I find myself upon the shelf
Where my love left it many years ago
Why she left it there I still do not know

What I learn from looking too long inside:
Too much introspection one cannot abide

A Song of Shakespeare

William Shakespeare wrote many a sonnet
Dedicated to a close noble friend
His lady wore a bright summer bonnet
Which she did fancy to a bitter end

Her sweet love belonged to the number two
It was destined to be broken apart
For it does not matter how right it seems
One is the number of a faithful heart

It was such sweet pleasure while it lasted
They believed it would last quite forever
But when moments of pain came to test them
That which bound them together did sever

So remember whenever you're lonely
Love will never belong to you only

The Good and the Great

To create masterworks of art is great
To acknowledge them is good
To affect enduring change is great
To nurture a child is good
To build a lasting legacy is great
To greet each day with kindness good

We are taught to admire greatness
To bow down before bronze statues
To pay tribute to the classics
To praise the golden sun
But not the common one

We strive our entire lives
To rise and do great things
But is it the good that matters most
It is the voice that sings
It is the good that touches the heart
It is the truth that rings
We cannot all reach greatness
But we can keep it in our sight
We can hold it to our bosoms
To give comfort through the night

Being Here

(Song of Self II)

In the morrow we awake without fear
We refuse to look beyond where we are
Nor will we look back at days left behind
We may wander but we will not go far

We exist in the moment eternal
We will live our lives in the here and now
We will offer blessings for all that is
We will welcome what the fates allow

For there is no force in all the heavens
That can tell us what to and not to do
As long as we remain in the moment
And treasure each day as if it were new

We spend too much of our time in worry
Relax take it easy and don't hurry

Decisions

(A Song of Choice)

Here's some advice when you're caught in a vice
When in doubt you must make a decision
There are times to rely on gut feelings
There are times you must seek a new vision

Too often our minds take us in circles
The Dane's dilemma will lead us astray
While tomorrow could bring a new answer
The same answer may be given today

Don't spend too much time in circular rhyme
It's as bad as investing too little
For a choice that seems sound in the morrow
May in time become broken and brittle

When it comes to all difficult matters
Too many thoughts can make reason shatter

Homeward

(A Song of Home)

The warmth and comfort of home now beckons
Though it has been but a moment in time
The minutes drag on like an old love song
That is fastened to the edge of your mind

We have paid our debt to our memories
We have journeyed to the family heart
Now we wish them well and we say goodbye
In our soul of souls we're never apart

Our hearts are teeming with comfort and joy
As we embark on the journey once more
Our past behind us our future ahead
We close a chapter and open a door

We must always honor these journeys past
For we never know which will be our last

Echo Chamber

Voices without ears
Shouts that rumble in all directions
Reverberating like an overheated amplifier
Bouncing off the walls floor and ceiling
Building momentum increased velocity
Seeking shelter where none exists
Alpha without omega
Would be leaders without followers
Volume multiplying volume
Forces compounding forces
Building to an unsustainable mass
Until the chamber finally shatters
Leaving only disparate voices
Scattered and indecipherable
Like broken glass
Voices without ears

By the River

My legs pull me down to the riverside
Where the brush is thick as tulle fog
Where the scent of river life explodes
Where all things dead and alive
Rust decay and revive
Nourishing the cycle of life

Down by the river life is brutal and cold
Down by the river the seasons sing
Bright and beautiful and bold
Take me down to the river
When I am tired longing and old

I saw a bird lain on the ground
Sparkling feathers blue and gold
A tiny lifeless bundle
Spoke of glory now untold

I saw a coyote on the prowl
Its life sustained through fair and foul
It takes the lesser beings
To feed the river's thirst
So teeming with life and wonder
I thought my soul would burst

My legs pull me down
To see these sights
To know these sacred truths
That all things living are dying
And all things dead give life

(for Chris Mansel)

Multiplicity

The duality of man
The trinity of spirit
The multiplicity of the human mind
The singularity of soul
The individuality of humankind

I am but one man
With five to seven senses
Infinite in thought
Infinite imagination
Finite in emotion
Finite comprehension

I stand on the history of all
Who laid their tracks before me
I walk beside them on the path
I stand before the fall

I know everything
I know nothing at all
The universe beckons
I answer the call

Too many voices can kill
The creative process
A singularity of voice
Most certainly will

I have heard the voices of antiquity
I have welcomed them into my soul
I have distinguished between mythology

Methodology and philosophy
With all this I have grown old

I am not who I was as a young man
And yet I am
I was bolder then
And yet I am far bolder now
I am wiser now
And yet I was wiser then

I am all these things
Yet I am none
I am many things
Yet I am one

Would I cut off my arm to spite my hand?
Would I sever my soul to free my spirit?

I am the multitudes
I am the one
I am unity
I am none

Solidarity

When we march we are one
One cause one movement one mind
There is no space between us
We will not get out of line

When we think we are one
Separate independent and apart
We march to the same rhythm
We feel with distinct hearts

When it comes to bringing change
Solidarity is an essential thing
But when it comes to free expression
Let us find a voice that sings

To the music in our souls
To the thunder in our ears
Let us find the voice that sings
If it takes a thousand years

Listen

Those who talk must also listen
Those who shout must also hear
For though we value honest words
Those who listen we hold most dear

There was once a man of high esteem
Who talked in endless circles
But no one welcomed his company
Not even Angela Merkel

Apologies to that great woman
She listens with the best
But there are many in high places
That would put you to the test

This world is cursed with too much talk
Too few who choose to listen
The talk-a-lots are dull and plain
Good listeners fairly glisten

Friends Abroad

I have a friend in jolly old
Who knows which way the wind blows
He puts his finger in the air
And senses who does and does not care

I have a friend in the world below
Over time we've watched it grow
She has a keen and supple mind
I count on her to be most kind

For that's what true friendships do
They find a voice that comforts you
And though they give more than they get
I am most grateful to have met

Such true and gracious friends abroad
Their words I treasure and applaud
I think of them most every day
Though they remain so far away

(for Cal Wenby)

The Rain

I was sullen dour lulled
By the dullness of days
Into a passive hollow laze
Of melancholy madness
Prolonged silent sadness
In my soul

Then the rains came
To wash away my maze
Of perpetual malaise
The fog and endless haze
Of melancholy madness
Prolonged silent sadness
In my soul

The universe now glistens
As I listen to the rain
As it washes through my brain
Like a locomotive train
On the tracks to the city
Where the women are all pretty
And the men are pretty wise
If you ask they will advise
Stop the madness
End the sadness
In your soul

Then the rains came down
And washed it all away
It begins again today
In my soul

Love & The Wind

Love is like the wind
It caresses you on a summer day
Whispers gently in your ear
Teases you with laughter
Sings memories of carefree times
Then it turns on you in fits of rage
It knocks you to your knees
And leaves you begging
For sweet mercy

Love is like the wind
It defies your wit and wisdom
It pushes at your destiny
It drains your strength
Defeats you and forgives you
Soothes and depletes you
Draws you far away from home
And pulls you back again
Love is like the wind

(Note: When I first encountered Pablo
Neruda's Love Poems in Spanish, I
misinterpreted the title (Viente Poemas)
as wind poems (viento poemas).)

Broken

Something is wrong
Something is out of place
As if a foreign object
Has occupied a familiar space

I go about my business
As I have always done
But when I reach the end
I find I've just begun

I'm running in circles
Around and around and around
But something that's lost
Will never again be found

Two steps forward
Three steps back
An accelerating train
Will outrun its tracks

We are broken
Scattered in pieces
Retracing our path until
Momentum ceases

Song of Solstice

(Winter is Here)

The days become short and the nights so long
Our hearts are ringing with the sound of song
A northern chill has invaded the air
A winter darkness sweeps us in its lair

We have no true longing to venture out
Deep winter shadows fill our minds with doubt
Frost covers the ground and the air grows still
The marrow of bones senses winter's chill

The season of death descends upon all
The heavens in mourning after the fall
We burrow ourselves inside our warm homes
And give thanks to all we are not alone

We endure this winter of discontent
And contemplate where our adventures went

Song of Fate

Creatures of habit believers in fate
Hold on through the night pray it's not too late
We accept our gods lead us on this path
We trust we have not earned the gods' cruel wrath

We live each moment no planning ahead
No need for emotion nothing to dread
We place our whole lives in fate's solid hands
And trust where we're meant is where we will land

For fate holds the keys that open the doors
That guides us to harbors on distant shores
That tempts us to err that leads us astray
That in the end sees that we find our way

The fates and the muses live in the air
They let us believe and spur us to dare

Destiny

If we have a purpose and a soul
Then surely we have a destiny
A longing that pulls at our heartstrings
A yearning that never lets go

When destiny calls we must answer
Be it writer musician or dancer
That feeling deep down in our hearts
That leads us to science or arts

But when we cast our fate to the wind
We know only where it begins
Where it ends we cannot know
We set our course and there we must go

It can be hard to follow a calling
It requires much hardship and falling
But we always get up and press on
As our destiny drives us along

Doves

No one can speak for my people
All of my friends are tight
We never turn on each other
When others oppose us
    we will fight

No one should mess with my family
We share a bond of love
We will look out for each other
A light of protection
    from above

A circle of love surrounds us
Holding us all inside
A spirit of warmth will guide us
Where we were meant to go
    we will find

We know it won't last forever
Though we would want it to
In time we may find another
Person or place to go
    that is true

Joy

Let all hardship and worry go
Today is a day of joy
It is a time of winter wonder
For the children and their toys

Let go the lingering discontent
Let go the tears of rage
Forgive betrayal and transgression
On vengeance turn the page

Tonight there is no sorrow
There is no fear or dread
There is only cheer and happiness
As we lay our souls to bed

Tomorrow we awaken
To a world of many wonders
A world where joy and faith
Cast misery asunder

Merry Christmas

Merry Christmas to lovely Lily
As she wakes on Christmas morn
Among her many presents
May she love her unicorn

Merry Christmas to Ellie and Addie
How they love their mom and daddy
We hope their wishes all come true
For this world was made for you

Merry Christmas little Logan
He fills the room with joy
And all the world is blessed to be
In the presence of this little boy

Merry Christmas to our Grayson
He is in our hearts to stay
He smiles and frowns and clowns around
What joy to watch him play

Merry Christmas to Zendaya
She makes her father sigh
She sings her heart and dances
Like a proud young colt prances

[MERRY XMAS TO ALL!
But especially the little ones!]

Music City

I remember Christmas in Nashville
A city bursting with excitement
Where every person you met
Was a singer or a song
Where country paid the rent
But every kind of muse was alive

I remember the poetry scene
(down on Second Street as I recall)
Dancing to a hard rock beat
Paying tribute to the bards of old
And the beats of San Francisco
Infused with jazz rock and folk
A town that welcomed all to its fold

I remember Nashville in the round
A city of dreams and dreamers
Characters in search of a story
Singers in search of a song
Poets in search of rhyme

Nashville at Christmas time
When everyone put their dreams aside
And embraced the spirit of being
A spirit of sharing and giving
A spirit of friendship and trust

To see it all come crashing down
At the hands of some random madman
Is almost beyond forgiving

(an explosion stuns Nashville on Christmas)

Vengeance III

Vengeance is the seed of evil deeds
Even more so than hate or greed
To seek vengeance is to forego grief
So that sorrow vengeance feeds

We all suffer loss and heartbreak
We feel that vengeful yearning
But our wiser selves will overcome
To understand our need for learning

For vengeance feeds more vengeance
And violence is answered in kind
Until the whole world is set ablaze
And virtues fall behind

Far better to let our anger go
To let it run its course
Than to get entangled in a maze
And mired in remorse

We place our faith in knowing
That justice will find a way
The guilty will be punished
That dog will have its day

Patience

The sins all have their contraries
Like the blessed virtue patience
In these days of endless suffering
We're learning to be latent

But the walls of worry surround us
Like a prison of our own devise
It tests our will and stamina
Our desire to be wise

It's so hard to maintain reason
When all we have is time
We spend the hours contemplating
And devising novel rhymes

Thank god the old are still around
To teach us patience' worth
For patience is most necessary
To enable our rebirth

Killer Drugs

450,000 dead and rising
Year after year after year
While we weren't watching
While our eyes were fixed to the killer virus
The killer drugs did not disappear
They continued their march of death
Spreading north to south east to west
Oxycontin Vicodin fentanyl
Sounding a heartless death knell
The curse of the pharmaceuticals
The scourge of a drug abuse nation
An act of virtual annihilation
The ravages of blatant greed
To satisfy the money breed
Death by invitation

What more do we need to take
The money out of medicine?

Fosdick & Muldoon

(Play Series)

He is one who knows not what he wants
Nor how to get what he thinks he wants
He cannot be even superficially happy

I marvel at how one so young
Should fall so short of optimum
On the scale of hope and faith
Makes all the senses go numb

And along comes Fosdick
Just short of a buffoon
To offer up a counterpoint
To the cynical Muldoon

Round and round and round they go
The reasons for living on
Pride fulfillment happiness
An old familiar song

They argue to the end of time
And wind back home again
For though they reach a climax
They can never reach the end

(D'Arc Underground and
Other Plays by Jack Random)

The Ringed Women

(Play Series)

Ringed women of the forbidden forest
The numbers four and seven
Earth wind rain and fire
A place next door to heaven

Our hero must survive the test
For seven days and seven nights
He cannot sleep he cannot rest
Till he completes the seven rites

In the end he will succeed
By remaining just and true
When he meets the one he loves
He knows what he must do

The two are joined together
An enemy to kill
Freedom reigns throughout the land
The prophecy fulfilled

(Aphrodite House and Other Plays
By Jack Random)

Aphrodite House

(Play Series)

A dream of romantic love
Unbound eternal love
A house of magic
The embodiment of woman
The soul of Aphrodite
Goddess of sensual love
Mother of Eros
She spins her web
And lovers fall

But Aphrodite gives love to many
And jealousy to all she touches
Her blessing is a curse
The sweet nectar of her love
Turns bitter and blue

Something gained and something lost
Love prevails but at a cost

(Aphrodite House and Other Plays
By Jack Random)

The Bomber

He wanted to be remembered
Beyond that we don't know why
He had no cause or other motive
He had suffered no loss to justify

If he was bitter he didn't say
He didn't want to kill or maim
The word he left before his deed
He wanted us to say his name

So let's agree from this time forward
He was a bomber and nothing more
The stuff of life no longer pleased him
Disillusioned to the core

Let academics shuffle through his brain
We will only know his shame
He was the man who bombed Christmas
He is the man who will not be named

Here's to the Fallen

We lost a lot of heroes this year
The older we get the quicker they fall
Like asteroids from the heavens
Childhood memories and legends
Singers and songwriters
Poets and playwrights
Athletes and adventurers
Artists and scientists
Faces we'd almost forgotten
Names at the tips of our tongues
People we placed on a pedestal
Pictures on a calendar
Photos on the wall

And yet nearly all of us
Are heroes to someone
The kind and the gentle
The generous and wise
An elder who cheered you on
A teacher who gave you comfort
A relative who encouraged you
Someone you loved

Here's to the fallen heroes
May they live forever in our hearts
May they thrive in our memories
May they survive the test of time

Snake Pit Slam

A curse upon your house and city
A curse upon your dreams
May vipers slither in your psyche
May they settle in your schemes
May they make a home inside your head
And burrow in your legacy

May you lose your moral mooring
May you drift out to open sea
Where seven waves and seven ports
Consume your sensibilities
And push you to the brink of gone
Where you decay with dark disease

May you walk without direction
May you find no place to be
May you be lost in mindless wandering
Cursing everyone you see
May they curse you back again
As you surrender willingly

The Mulligan

The big man played a round of golf
With me and Ned Divine
If that's the way you play says I
A mulligan is fine
But if you're playing round with us
You'll place us in a bind
We'll give you one or two old man
But we cannot give you nine

So the big man comes back again
And wants to play a round
Twas me and Ned and someone said
We'll have to turn you down
Not only did you falsely claim
To beat both Ned and me
But you took my favorite Brassie
And tossed her in the sea

Mira Mar

Listen to the voice of the deep blue sea
Angry or sullen she comforts me

The awesome breadth and depth of power
Bolsters me in the darkest hour

She waves her wand and casts her spell
Assuring me all will be well

I breathe the air and count the waves
Silence the screams discount the raves

I cast my fortune into the sea
And know her voice will comfort me

The Mentor

We met the year I turned forty
Though I doubt he remembers
Life was exploding then
And I was exploding with it

We were Kerouac and Moriarty
On the road to enlightenment
He was Whitman and Yeats
A cut above our groove
Though we did not know it then

We sought him out for answers
As seekers do a wise man
He had only questions
A sense of joy and wonder
A taste for living and life
A drive for creative expression
A giving spirit

He welcomed us into his home
Entertained us with stories
Charmed us with wit and wisdom
Over Chinese at a local diner

We thanked him and went our way
Grateful for his conversation
Assured by his confidence
We had touched the hand of greatness
And gathered fuel for the journey

It would be twenty-seven years

Before we'd meet again
Not in person but on social media
Sharing words and poetry
Thoughts and speculations
The wisdom of his years
The sanctity of mine

My journey is different now
I have returned to poetry
After several lifetimes away
The world is not a welcome place
For those who roam and wander
We survive the great pandemic
And learn to dive within

He has become a mentor now
For I am ready to listen
For I am open to learning
For I am humbled by his mastery
Of form and substance
By his treasury of knowledge

He is a prophet of the multiverse
A disciple of the spoken word
A diviner of many voices
He touches minds and souls
Reaches distant plains of imagery
Captures yearning hearts
And pays tribute to the dead

He is a master poet
At a time there are so few
A legacy tethered to the stars
His word and heart are true

Patience II

The more we need it the less we have
We're willing to give it away
We'll sacrifice our future joy
For the want of patience today

As the sun sets on the western world
As the darkness settles in
As a swarm of worries surround us
And a chill creeps under our skin

As kids we want it all right now
As adults we learn to postpone
If we never grow up our tension rises
And never can we atone

Have patience my friend
There will come an end
Good things come to those who wait
Good women and men
On faith will ascend
Fulfillment will be their fate

Signs

The sun burns bright in Degas skies
Blooming flowers in an empty space
Clouds like dreams go swimming by
No smile or laugh seems out of place

Breath of angels on a crisp clear lake
A taste of light in the morning air
The mystic thoughts of William Blake
A sense that even strangers care

The rapture of the rising sun
We drink our joy in ample measure
The silence of a midnight run
Each breath becomes a treasure

We turn away from fearful times
And point our gaze ahead
Behold the many hopeful signs
Despair and gloom are dead

Omens

The heavy silence before a quake
Clouds of doom in midnight skies
A crack foretells a bridge's break
A glance reveals a scourge of lies

Thunder shakes us to the core
A pounding of torrential rain
The feeling we can take no more
Our senses numb before the pain

Three crows on a telephone line
A wrong turn down a darkened alley
My groove caught in a double bind
Vultures hover in a lonesome valley

We take each step with brooding care
A rolling fog betrays our eyes
Motionless we will not dare
Our fears take hold and rise

Crazy

When did crazy become cool?
When did cruel replace the golden rule?
Was there something in the water
Creating insane sons and daughters?
Was it something in the air?
Insurrection on a dare?
Was it something in the soil
That caused sanity to uncoil?
Was there something in the rays of sun
That left our decency undone?

We have arrived in an awkward place
An unraveling of the human race
The undoing of our moral core
An unleashing of the beasts of war
Revelation of destructive madness
Civilization yields pervasive sadness
And falls like a house of cards
Without walls and without guards

The Hole

There's a hole in my consciousness
Don't you know
There's a hole where I don't
Know what goes

There's a button in my shirt
That's always missing
There's a woman somewhere
I should be kissing

There's a hole in my vision
That I just cannot see
It's a hole through which someone
Is looking back at me

There's a hole in my mind
That turns my world around
Down becomes up
And up turns to down

There's a hole in my universe
I'll be damned if it's not true
There's a hole in my life
And I wonder if it's you

Soul Salvation

To believe in the soul
Is to believe in life beyond death
To believe that death is not real
To believe that death is but a moment
Of transition

To believe in salvation
Is to believe in judgement
To believe that a soul can be judged
Beyond the substance of a life
Beyond the summation of action
Beyond the essence of character and intent

To believe in soul salvation
Is to believe in eternal forgiveness
To believe in damnation
To believe in perfect wisdom
Beyond the reach of humankind

To believe in soul salvation
Is to accept the existence of god

Untamed Love

Love is not a sonnet
It cannot be tailored
To count or meter

There is no formula
No prescription
No form or structure
No handbook description

Love cannot be directed
It chooses it path
Like a river running
Through open land
It will not be controlled
It will not obey
It cannot be dammed

Love is the greatest blessing
When it chooses well
When a match it finds
When the giving is welcome
And returned in kind

My life is blessed by your love
As your life is blessed by mine

(for my love Julie Bradford)

Quiet

In the cool of the morning
You can hear the distant buzz
Of vehicles escorting workers
To their points of destination
If you listen quietly you can hear
The ghosts of vehicles past
The cars trains and buses
That roared like beasts of burden
So dominant they vanished
Into the symphony of noise

In the cool of the evening
If you listen with your mind
The part that stores memories
And dreams of things divine
You can hear the march of progress
Recede into the darkness
You can hear the beating heart
Of a new world in formation

Life Abundant

Industry technology
Medicine biology

The abundance of life sustains us
The limitations of life restrain us

The advent of industry
Alters the course of history
Mass centers of population
Assembly lines and labor stations
An explosion of the city state
Industry becomes our fate

The abundance of life sustains us
The limitations of life restrain us

The advance of technology
The age of mass psychology
Computers and the internet
The markets place your bet
The mind becomes supreme
Robotics run machines

The abundance of life sustains us
The limitations of life restrain us

The march of modern medicine
More healthy than we've ever been
Living ever longer lives
The medical profession thrives
The population grows

Our limitations show
We've pushed it to the edge
We're standing on a ledge

The abundance of life sustains us
The limitations of life restrain us

Our knowledge of biology
Genetic immunology
Our lives keep growing longer
Our bodies getting stronger
But there are toxins in the air
And the planet doesn't care

The abundance of life sustains us
The limitations of life restrain us

The Hype

The moment we've all waited for
A showdown for the ages
A match of the titans
The best of the best
In a test of all tests
The greatest of all time
Meets the latest in his prime
History in the making
The big ticket for the taking

But when the ads
Are better than the pads
And when the glow
Is brighter than the show
When you can phone it in
By the end of the half
It almost makes you laugh
It's all about the hype again
It's over well before the end

Raise your stein of beer
Can hardly wait for next year

Interesting Times

That old Chinese proverb:
You are blessed to live
In interesting times
Takes hold of my consciousness
A daily fixture in my mind

I hear so many complain
They are bored to death
Bored I think but not to death
Boredom doesn't kill
It may push you to folly
But it does not kill

We are cursed to live
In interesting times

We experience something new
And astonishing every day
Triumphs of medicine
The collapse of a glacier in India
The harshest storm in centuries
An epidemic of child poverty
In the world's richest nation
A phenomenon of mass hysteria
An upheaval in Russia
Insurrection in the USA

We are blessed to live
In interesting times
Indeed

Adventures of a Creative Life

I wander through this life
Of one mind determined
An inspiration to find
My thirst is for beauty
My hunger is for love
My desire is for creativity
Inspired from above

There is no other longing
That drives my inner soul
A thirst for art
A hunger for romance
A quest for creation
A part in the dance

Every breath and every move
Is directed at one goal
To uncover the secrets
That will make me whole
That will still my restless heart
That will alter my core
That will set my direction
And define my role

Art is everything
The yin and the yang
The Zen and the epiphany
The solution to the mystery
Hearing the higher call
The moment of understanding
The answer to it all

I wander through this life
Knowing there are no answers
There is no destination
There is no moment of perfection
There is only the adventure
The seeking and the goal
The quest for the answer
That makes my life whole

Screen Fatigue

My friend from Florence
Grows tired of the screen
Big screens little screens
Screens of all makes and sizes
Have outworn his patience

He is a master artist poet
Analyst and philosopher
I wonder what it means
When the best of my generation
Rejects the constant data stream

Is it rotting our minds
Is it distorting our vision
Is it destroying our sensibilities
And perverting our dreams

We know we cannot reverse time
We cannot stop the river flowing
We can only control ourselves
Our exposure and abuse
We can only mitigate damage
By limiting our use

We know we cannot know the harm
If we ourselves are victims
We cannot destroy the disease
If we only know the symptoms

History Aforethought

If you could see these events
Through the telescope of time
A century removed from now
When the passion has long subsided
When the partisan divide is tempered
When we've healed the great divide
Would we see things differently
Would we alter our actions
Would we take another look

If we could read history's verdict
Would we see the great betrayal
With new and open eyes

If we could hear history's decree
Would it alter our perspective
If Benedict Arnold knew he would
Live in eternal infamy
If Jefferson knew he would not be
Forgiven his crimes and misdeeds
If Sirhan and Oswald knew
They were being played for fools
If the Germans knew how it ended
If the South knew would they defend it
Would they sacrifice all dignity and pride
If they knew they were on the losing side

Would things be different today
Or would we just continue on
This march of shame

The Other Pandemic

McKinsey Consultants
For the pharmaceutical industry
Helped propagate a deadly scourge
Long before the virus came
And the song became a dirge

They deliberately spread
The opioid addiction
Profit over principle
Death with conviction

Purdue Pharma
Avarice incorporated
Promoting oxycontin
As a universal cure
A pusher with pedigree
The ultimate lure

The doctors who went along
As if they didn't know better
Passing out prescriptions
To create a trendsetter

All the people who died
What does it really matter
People die all the time
And the fat are getting fatter

Simple

Nature embraces the simple *
The spider's web reveals
A most elegant design
Sturdier than any invented
By the human mind

The forest canopy displays
The conversion of sunlight
To life sustaining energy
For an entire universe
Of complex and interrelated
Systems beyond our device

From the smallest entity
To the infinite galaxies
In the farthest corners
Of our observational minds
Nature is our finest teacher
If only we would listen
And act in kind

We are simple beings
No matter how complex it seems
From the deepest mystery
To our most fantastic dreams
Driven by basic needs
Central to survival
Like planting seeds

* Tom Paine in The Age of Reason

Floating Thoughts

Dark clouds in the northern sky
Clear skies overhead
Today we begin a new life
Another chapter to be read

We know not what the future holds
Be it promise or demise
We take what destiny unfolds
Revealed by our own two eyes

If past is prelude to the days ahead
Great hardship we will endure
Tears of sadness will be shed
Loss and mourning are assured

But days of wonder will also bless
Our lives with awesome bliss
The young at heart we will invest
And happiness we will enlist

The Blank

The ability of the mind to see
Whatever we might want to be
To mold and bend reality
To shape it to our will
To make the river still
The empty glass to fill
    and drink

We are living in a dream
Not caring what it means
Tearing at the seams
We walk our lonely roads
Disguising what it shows
And hiding what we know
    to be true

We're filling in the blanks
While offering our thanks
To all within the ranks
Of those who do not care
Who fix their eyes and stare
While sitting in their chairs
    of comfort

We must find another way
To greet the light of day
To guide a lamb that strayed
To find our way back home
No more to blindly roam
Like children left alone
    and lost

Eyes

I greet the day with eyes wide open
I wonder and amaze
What fabulous events will unfold
To mystify or enchant me
What illuminating tales will be told
I am the receiver of golden promise
My senses are tuned to raise
I am the witness to the story
My eyes behold the daze
I see what others cannot see
Perceived beyond the phase
A world in liquid motion
A time of wicked lies
A place of pure devotion
A wonder to my eyes

The waters breathe and take it in
Air flows in waves of power
The earth below our humble feet
Churns in transformation
Fire rules the sky and soothes
The planet even as it burns
Life reveals itself at every turn
We breathe it in and learn

These eyes these ears this heart this mind
Are blessed with everything we find
As we await that final night
That final breath that ends our flight

Sweat

Seven sacred stages
Seven waves of spirits rising
I felt the breath of death
I saw their many faces
I sensed my spirit lift and hover
In the mist above the stones
As if it was decided

The stones the sweat the taste of salt
Imploding visions in clouds of fog
The past becomes the present
The future naked and exposed
I saw their faces
I felt my spirit rise
I smelled the breath of death

The ghosts of seven ages
Spoke to me then
They sing to me now
In words I cannot translate
But know and understand
Seven waves seven stages
The seven tribes of man

Counting Fear

The people whom fear counted
Were a tough and hardy crew
Some roamed the streets in hunger
Some on raven's wings flew
Who will answer the cry for help
Who will come to Waterloo
Curses reign in skies of thunder
Waves of darkness will ensue
Blessings count the fortunate
Honor counts the few
Desperation counts the weary
Dignity counts the true
Of the people whom fear counted
There were many like me and you
Of those whom fear passed over
There is nothing we can do

(for Maryanna Gabriel)

Emirates on Mars

There are hogs in high heaven
Butterflies in the stars
Beauty is wearing a mask
And the Emirates landed on Mars

Few knew they had an interest
In exploring the world from afar
But they have an abundance of money
So they used it to land on Mars

What more will the Emirates do
Mass produce a green energy car
Attack poverty and ban slave labor
Promote poetry enlightenment art

Whatever the future may promise
Lightning is caught in a jar
Possibilities have no limits when
The Emirates have landed on Mars

The Grudge

For as long as memory holds
I have held a grudge against
The great state of Texas
The state that gave us George Dubya Bush
And the never-ending wars
The state that gave us Enron
As its energy consortiums skimmed
Billions upon billions from California
Oregon and Washington

I have held a grudge against Texas
For holding back progress
For mass incarceration
For climate change denial
For immigration hypocrisy
For corporate corruption
For institutional inequality
For a cowboy mentality

I have held a grudge against Texas
For Lee Harvey Oswald
The book depository
And the infamous grassy knoll
(who could ever forget
the grassy knoll?)

I held onto that grudge a long time
Before I realized
The grudge was holding onto me
Before I understood
People are pretty much the same

Texans are not to blame
So much as greed
And hatred
And envy
And the need for revenge
The need to be better than
Foolish Texas pride
(not so different than California's)
It's the way we were raised
What we learned in school
What our parents handed down
Along with family photos
Stories and fairy tales

We were taught the ways of war
Of us versus them
Of good against bad
Of north against south
Of east against west
Red against blue
And black against white
But somewhere along the way
We picked up empathy
When the quake hit LA
It shook us all
When Paradise went up in flames
We all cried
When tornadoes ripped across
The Oklahoma plains
We shared the horror
When Katrina struck New Orleans
We all suffered
When the towers fell
We all mourned

Now Texas feels the blow

Of a relentless winter storm
And Texas is not alone
We must all carry the burden
We are Americans
We are humans
We are inhabitants of a small planet
We are one

We Will Overcome

We are backed against the wall
A pit of vipers at our feet
Outnumbered and outgunned
We are staring at defeat
But we strengthen our resolve
As the battle is not done
We swear on all that's sacred
We will overcome

From a summer of blazing fire
To the winter of the freeze
We can hardly remember when
Our lives were blessed with ease
We have endured the great pandemic
We will survive the next disease
Fire wind ice and thunder
An explosion of the sun
Whatever nature nurtures
We will overcome

The preachers cry for mercy
Prophets hang their heads
Undertakers prosper
Soldiers count the dead
Poverty is everywhere
The peasants have no bread
The glory days are finished
No more battles to be won
Yet when the day turns over
We will overcome

Stupid and Proud

I'm stupid and proud
I'll say it real loud
I'm stupid and I'm proud

I've been around since the crucible
I marched in the first crusade
I cheered the first emperor
I bowed to the first king
I died for Napoleon
I lied for Rasputin
I saluted the Roman conquerors

When it comes to reason
I'm not well endowed
I'm stupid and I'm proud

I lit the fire that burned Chicago down
Sacrificed my first born son
Applauded the torture of witches
I fought against unions
I fought against Indians
I fought in the trenches
Of all the old wars
I fought against equal rights

In every decade of every century
I'm the one who follows the crowd
I'm stupid and I'm proud
I'll say it again real loud
I'm stupid and I'm proud

Envy

I envy those who breathe
The crisp ocean air
Outside their window
Every morning at sunrise
Every evening at twilight
To hear the pounding waves
The soothing ebb and flow
Of life sweet salty life

Oh that I were there
To breathe the ocean air
What would I give?
What would I dare?

I envy those who greet the day
With the scent of mountain pines
The coolness of Sierra peaks
The promise of fresh snow
Clear lakes and rivers flow
The people of the mountains
Are kind but tough
The pace of life is slow

Oh that I were there
To breathe the mountain air
What would I give?
What would I dare?

I envy those who live the city life
Where lives collide in a cacophony
Of light and sound and energy

Where the beat pounds the pavement
Where jazz rules the night
Where boredom never settles
And the hustle never rests

Oh that I were there
To breathe the city air
What would I give?
What would I dare?

I envy those who live the valley life
The fruit of hard labor
The salt of the giving earth
Where the seasons gently turn
And the almond blossoms bloom
Where the mountains are in view
And the coast is near enough
To taste and savor

Oh that I were there
To breathe the valley air
What would I give?
What would I dare?

Ferlinghetti

"If you would be a poet,
create works capable of answering
the challenge of apocalyptic times."

Lawrence Ferlinghetti
Poetry as Insurgent Art

He fought the endless battle
For justice and equality
For peace and integrity
For art and creativity
With passion through poetry

He asked us to Speak Out
From our hearts to change minds
With our arts and our many voices
He was strong but always kind

He knew it was a battle
That would not end
Not in his lifetime or mine
He knew it was the fight
That mattered most
The constant state of struggle
That keeps the heart pumping
That keeps the ball rolling
That keeps the march marching
That in the end tells the story
Of humankind

He was the keeper of the beat
Holder of the sacred torch
Bearer of the golden flame
An institution of the City
Protector of the Lights
The banner of a generation
Passed through his hands
And settled in his soul

(Lawrence Ferlinghetti, Poet Extraordinaire,
Founder of City Lights; born in Bronxville NY,
March 24, 1919, died SF, February 22, 2021.)

The Last Beat

The Beats arrived in the fifties
And stayed till the last call
The last stanza
The last howl
The last trip in a magic bus
The last hitch down a lonesome highway
The last snap and the last sigh

The Beats stole poetry
From the literary crowd
Gave it to the people
To start a whole new scene

Don't hide it on the shelf
Don't polish it like brass
Break down all the fences
Sing it out!
Sing it loud!

The Beats laid down a legacy
Of wonderment and rage
Of righteous indignation
The birthright of an age

They gave a promise to their elders
No longer to be quiet
No longer to be content
No longer to be satisfied
With three square meals a day
A roof and a lawn

They broke down convention
For an entire generation

Rise up and be counted!
Rise up and be rude!
Resist the days of comfort
Assume a restless attitude

The bow tie and bouffant crowd
Despised them for their youth
Despised them for their dissidence
Despised them for their cool
But the kids loved them
And celebrated their liberation
With a taste of their own

The song is winding down now
The last beat is sounding
The hipsters are not around now
But their spirits live on
Their drumbeat reverberates
In the echoes of our minds
Their call to the arms of poetry
Their rebel soul will never die

Cry for A Vision

Crazy Horse went into the hills
To cry for a vision
I cry with Crazy Horse

Crazy Horse received seven visions
He might have received nine
I cry for a vision that is
Mine and only mine

Crazy Horse was a visionary
I am all but blind
Yet I have seen my life
In many places
Many spaces many times

I have been the coyote
I have been the crow
I have been the wolf
I have been the buffalo
I have been the fire
I have been the stone
I have been the rain
I have been the snow

There is nothing in this life
I have not seen
There is nothing in this life
I have not been

It is here
It is gone

It is always
It is done

When I awake
I will carry my vision
Into the waking world
When I sleep I will return
To the home in my dreams

A Life

What is a life if not a book
If not a story
If not a portrait
If not a poem

What is a life if not a song
Sung by a troubadour
From across the sea
A thousand years before

What is a life if not
A mountain to be climbed
A race to be run
A triumph to be claimed
A loss to be endured
Before the setting of the sun
Before the journey is done

What is a life without death
A dream without substance
A dance without rhythm
A feast without wine
A love without passion
A wait without time

Life is the adventure
Without which there are no others
And death is her constant companion
The shadow of her soul
That which makes her whole

Rejoice and savor every moment
Every drop and every wisp of air
Every stroll through the garden
Every chance to do or dare

What is a life if not
Everything and more

Vertigo

The earth beneath my feet
Becomes an unsettled mass
An ever-shifting wave of sand
The rotation of the planets
A fault in the field of play

Cannot move forward
Cannot move back
The ever-spinning universe
Stills me in my tracks

The ever-spinning universe
Drills into my head
Pulls me to the waiting earth
Places me in bed

No longer can I stand upright
Like any other man
For fear vertigo will strike
And fold the solid land

Tree of Life

I watch the wheel spin round and round
I wonder how we do not remember
I see the towers come crashing down
I think back on that day in September

They took a wrong turn
They made a bad choice
They followed a trail of lies
Now they've learned their lessons
Now they understand
They bow down before the tree of life

We have gone to war
We have fought the fight
To the gods of greed we have sacrificed
We have fought for money
We have fought for pride
We have fought pretending
God was on our side

We took a wrong turn
We made a bad choice
We followed a trail of lies
Now we've learned our lessons
Now we understand
We bow down before the tree of life

We have learned a hard truth
Now we realize
Playing follow the leader
It was never wise

If we want to grow
And we want to survive
We must value the planet
We must value all tribes
We bow down before the tree of life
We bow down before the tree of life

(Regards to the late John Prine)

Walking in Dreams

Floating through distant galaxies
Slowing light speed to a crawl
Exploring inner space and outer limits
Without any limits at all

Diving to the deepest depths
Where the liquid darkness concealed
Creatures beyond imagining
Its hidden mysteries revealed

Rise above the mountains
Soar across the seven seas
Revisit those who left this earth
And return with a sense of ease

We are the gods of our existence
When we walk in our dreams
No adventure beyond our reach
No experience beyond our means

The Fruits of Labor

The rise of industry transformed the land
Controlling workers with an iron hand
Organized labor transformed the nation
Offering workers a glimpse of salvation

The wealthy hit the unions so hard
Workers feared to carry a union card
But it's time to tell the truth at last
The unions built the middle class

Our parents knew the hardship
Of working for a heartless boss
Their parents knew the blessings
Before the unions lost

So if you hold the enduring dream
Of a bright and better world for all
Rebuild the labor movement
Before the unions fall

A Giving Heart

Love never dies
Beauty is eternal
Kindness endures the ages
The giving spirit always gives
The soul within always lives

Those who know her mourn today
A sorrow in the heart of all
For that which she gave in kindness
Today is returned in grief

Yet we possess the comfort she endowed
The comfort knowing her eyes still see
Her voice still sings
Her ears still listen
Her mind still reasons
Her heart still beats
Her love and kindness still gives
Though now her body cannot suffer
The pain that ran through her bones
Vanished with the setting sun

She mourns our mourning
She grieves our grief
She suffers our mortal suffering
But the pain is gone

Her love lives forever
Her giving heart endures
And those who know and love her
Will remember her
Always

Remember

We remember in our hearts
We remember in our bones
We remember in the words we choose
We remember in the choices we make
We remember in each step we take

I cannot help but wonder
What others may remember
A hundred years from now

Will they remember your smile
Preserved in an ancient image
Reflected in a loved one's phrase
Captured on a poet's page

Will they remember your love
And how you gave it so freely
Will they remember your generosity
Will they remember your empathy

Will your spirit still exist
In the consciousness of others
Will they rise to your memory
And raise a toast to your living soul

I believe they will remember
Though they may not have a name
For that strange sense of wonder
That lifts us from our shame

For we live forever

Not only in the heart and mind
But in the air the trees the soil
The misty ocean and the tides

I will remember you
As I hope you remember me
For time is but an illusion
In a vast and endless sea

(in memory of Julie Brughelli)

Old Songs

Every man woman and child
Is born to a natural rhythm
A rhythm that guides our every step
Through a long and varied life

We remember the songs
That harmonize our natural rhyme
That drum to our beating hearts
That sing to the rhythm of our souls

Old songs pick us up
When we're down and stumbling
Old songs serenade us in love
And guide us on our journeys
Of the heart

Old songs are in our bones
They come to us when we need them
They sing to us and tap our toes
They bring us back to old times
When we were young and vibrant
When the universe opened to our door
And life's promises would never end
Old songs are old friends

Old songs keep us strong and alive
With hope and memories
We call them to us and they answer
Without fail

The Big Hustle

Go to school
Get a college degree
Enter the working force with skills

Four to eight years of hard study
Only to emerge deeply in debt
They seize your earnings
They destroy your financial health
You can't get a loan
You can't buy a home
They own you for life

There is no escape
They took away the options
They block you at every turn
Welcome to virtual debtor's prison
They grab you by the balls
And wonder how you could be so dumb

It's the big hustle
And if it lessens the sting
Don't worry: you're not alone

Accumulation

We are all that we have ever been
We are every moment of doubt
We are every breath of affirmation
We are what we are without
We are the love our mother gave us
We are the strength our father drove
We are an explosion of anger
We are the spirit of resolve
We are that awkward haircut in the seventh grade
We are the underdog who overcame
We are the hand that helped a stranger
We are the times we turned away
We are the music and the dance
We are the stumble and the fall
We are everything we ever thought
We are everything we ever saw
We are everything we ever felt
And everything we ever dreamed
We are fantasies of pure illusion
And everything they seem
We are that for which we are not proud
And that we should not have said out loud
We are everything we have ever done
We are joyful laughter and endless fun
We are the thoughts we take to bed
We are all that rambles through our heads
We are everything we've thrown away
We are the place we chose to stay

We are an accumulation of all things
Within our sphere of understanding
And beyond

The Bridge

You're young and healthy
(at least you think you are)
If you believe you can jump off a bridge
Without harm to yourself or others
I'm fine with that
Live free or die
Do what you will
Go your own way
Dance to your own music

But don't go berserk
If I won't do the same
Your freedom does not include
The right to bully me
Your rights do not trump mine

I must admit the fact that you endanger
Others with your recklessness
Bothers me

It drills into my consciousness
And triggers my rejection

Do unto others is my creed
(I thought it was yours)
I thought we were all in this together
Until we weren't

So go ahead
Jump off that bridge
Just don't take anyone with you

Relief

Sigh breathe take it in let it go
Like shelter from a winter storm
Like fire in a world of snow
At last relief is on the way
To soften hardship's blow

A billion words in Washington
Without a word of common sense
Without a sign of understanding
Without a hint of recompense

But in the end the ones
Who have no needs
Gave in to those who do
In the end their willful ignorance
Gave in to what is plainly true

The ones who lost their livelihoods
The ones who cannot pay the rent
The ones who live from day to day
The ones whose hope is all but spent

Spend an hour in their heads
Know their worries and their fears
No longer would you play your games
If you could feel behind their tears

Carry On

Wiser words were never said
A better song was never sung
Than those two words by four wise men
Crosby Stills Nash and Young

For we may suffer long and hard
And we may feel we can't go on
And we may tap the depths of sorrow
But we must rise to carry on

Every man and woman must endure
The loss of a dearly beloved
We are driven to a mad despair
And cry out loud to the stars above

But when our grief is fully spent
Our desperate hour is finally done
We find the courage to love again
And the strength to carry on

The Body

The body as a vehicle
For transit between worlds
The body as an instrument
For creative expression
The body as a machine
To serve a greater purpose
The body as a prison
To confine a wayward spirit
The body as a receiver
Of sensory pain and pleasure
The body as a mystery
A puzzle to unfold
The body as a castle
A protector of the soul

We are gifted with this body
For as long as we are here
Care for it and cherish it
For beyond the body's sustenance
We cannot know
We can only hope
We can only pray
In the end we can only be

The Royal Bloodline

The royal family has decreed
The royal bloodline must be pure
Should any prince plant a seed
Immediate expulsion is the cure

The royal house of Windsor
Goes back a thousand years
The queen upholds tradition
And commoners hold her dear

The darker side of aristocracy
Is race discrimination
The goal of every royal wedding
Is genetic purification

The royal family through the ages
Is white as purest snow
Is all the pageantry necessary?
The answer: clearly no

The Long Road Home

Once I was young and bold
I struck on my own
I reached out for adventure
I walked a long hard road
Made many a friend
As the saying goes
But I walked alone
So when they call my name
Let it be known
On the highway of life
I took the long way home

I am retired now
I've grown weary and old
Content to trace the lines
Of a tale already told
I have lived a full life
Love and sorrow I have known
I have endured hard times
Through it all I've grown
I have paid up my dues
And I've tried to atone
It has never been easy
On the long road home

A Hard Rain

A hard rain fell
It came down like Dante's hell
It pounded on the solid earth
It hit for all that it was worth
As if it cast a wicked spell
It washed away the hills and soil
Where the tallest of tall trees fell
It tightened up our mortal coil
It rattled through and out our brains
It struck like rolling thunder
Driving all the little kids insane
Leaving everyone in wonder
It drummed on my windows
Nearly knocking down my door
It arrived like the devil's wind
And burrowed to the core

I guess this is what the poet meant
Seeking shelter from the storm
It's a hard rain gonna fall
Like the pounding drums of war
And it's a hard rain a falling
With a promise ever more
So take cover anywhere you can
And stay out of the pouring rain
Or you may find your sense of wonder
Washing down the drain

Pressure

The body knows what to do
Tension blocks the path
Throws us off our course
Like a blow from nature's wrath

The mind knows where to go
But pressure distorts the way
Running hot and cold in measures
Finding penalties to pay

The way of life is silky smooth
For those who find the flow
By easing through the tension
And letting pressures go

For life is filled with pressures
No matter how you live
And there are always takers
No matter what you give

Adversity I

Adversity will hunt you down
Wherever you may be
Hiding in the deepest woods
Or across the Salton Sea

There is no man or woman
Who has refuge from the beast
Adversity will take you home
When you expect it least

I knew someone who danced through life
Like a dancer on the floor
Adversity took her by the hand
And cast her boat offshore

You may think you can handle anything
Who knows? Maybe you can
But when adversity comes calling
You'd better have a plan

You can't escape it in the dark of night
You can't defeat with the light
There is no creature large or small
For whom adversity has no call

The Puzzle

It goads at the senses
Gnaws at the mind
It grabs hold of your attention
To all else it makes you blind

There are always missing pieces
You can never reach the end
For every piece you put in place
The more the picture bends

Life itself is a puzzling mystery
A thousand questions without answer
Like a train without a railroad track
Like a dance without a dancer

But if life is like a puzzle
With no beginning and no end
Then we can step into the mystery
To find waiting family and friends

Mystery Friend

In the shadows of the evening
There lurks a mystery friend
She sings to me in gentle tones
Before my dream world ends

I've asked her not to comfort me
When so many are in need
Yet still she comes each evening
To plant her mystery seeds

I plead with her to go away
To haunt some other man
She folds her arms around me
So that I might understand

She lives inside a dream
That possesses only me
And when my days are at an end
My eyes will truly see

She is my guardian spirit
She is my mystery friend
And when my life is over
She will guide me round the bend

Lesser Gods

I am just a trifle odd
I have always been attracted
To the lesser of the gods

While others chose Atlas
And the almighty Zeus
I chose Prometheus
And the immortal Dr. Seuss

You might say that's strange
And you would not be wrong
But we can't all join the chorus
Of an old familiar song

Some may sing of Nietzsche
And some the mighty Freud
I would favor Steinbeck
And the King of Androids *

Just as there are greater gods
So there are greater minds
The children of the lesser kind
Take the gods they find

For all of us cannot be wise
Some of us are fools
Some lingered in the school yard
While others were being schooled

* Phillip K. Dick

Echoes

I hear the nightingale sing
Though I have never heard or seen
The nightingale in form or space
I represent the human race
Though I have never seen its face
I am the sum of all I see
Yet it remains a mystery
I am and yet I am not there
I do not see and yet I stare
For there are echoes everywhere
And that I cannot bear
For I am not my self
I am books upon a shelf
And on that shelf I shall remain
Until some figure dark and strange
Should dare to break the seal
My secret soul shall be revealed
Then bury it away
Where echoes cannot stay
Where echoes cannot stay

The Old Oak

They still call it a live oak
Though it is clearly dying
Its naked arms reach outward
In all seven directions
People have supported it with
Thick wires of steel that
Make it seem invented
A work of human hands
Though it is clearly one of nature's
Most magnificent creations
One of the tallest order
It has witnessed the best and
Worst of humankind
It has watched the parade of
Style and always changing fashion
It has laughed at human folly
It has roared at human error
It has shed its leaves
Over centuries of toil
It has seen the river break
Over its earthen banks and
Swallow the land beneath
It has stood its ground and
Steadied all around it
A home to hawks and eagles
A perch for crows and jays
A playground for squirrels
A refuge for creatures great and
Small and bountiful as nature
It tires of the mystery now and
Yearns for the peace of solitude

A shadow of its former glory
It is time to let go sleep and
Rise in live oak dreams

Slow and Easy II

Relax take it easy go slow
The more you listen
The more you know
All our lives it's go-go-go
At this stage of life
Let's take it slow

There once was a man
Who always hurried
His hair was long and
A little curly
He hustled here and
He hurried there
He made mistakes but
He did not care
Until he met someone
Who made a list
Of all the things in life
He missed

Now he's grown old
He has regrets
He gambled hard and
Placed his bets
In the end he wagered
All the time he bought
Was not nearly worth
The things he sought

Be calm my friend
Walk slowly on
In the blink of an eye
It will all be gone

Degradation

As one grows old
One's vision fades
Along with all the senses
One's touch a little cruder
One's smell a little dulled
One's taste a little less acute
One's hearing less than whole
But it is vision I notice most
And the blessing it bestows

As I grow old
I can look in the mirror without fear
For the rough edges are smoother
The ragged beard more stylish
The deep lines less sharply drawn
The worry far less bold

Yes I am old
But I am blessed to see
The one I used to be
Each day as I behold
The man in the mirror
Looking back at me

Keys

He tickles the keys
Like she wears her jewelry
Summoning sounds in a delicate stream
Like waterfalls in a dream

He follows her wherever she leads
She is his dancing muse
She takes him to the darkest night
And loses him in flight

She flows and glides as he
Spins his web
Painting landscapes of the mind
Where heaven is defined

She follows him where he must go
He is her playing muse
He guides her to a wondrous place
Outside of time and space

Together they will dance and play
Like children out of school
She will hide the mystery
And he will play the fool

Designated Madness

March is designated the month of madness
If madness was a vile ingested substance
That could be expelled on the day of fools
All would be well

But madness cannot be expelled
Like toxic bile in the stomach or intestines
It lingers like a cruel and tragic image
That invades the psyche and latches on
That stakes its claim to the soul

Madness is the way of men
Who fall in love with power
Madness is born of jealousy and hate
Madness is the way of the mob
The runaway horror of genocide
A compulsive belief in fate
Madness is a hundred years of war
And men who yearn for a hundred more
Madness is belief without conviction
Conviction without substance
The stuff of dream and fancy
Without regard for the solid earth

We have survived years of madness
(some would say centuries)
We do not need a designated month
A designated year
A designated time for the sane to fear

Let madness thrive on its own device

It needs no help from man
Let us designate a month of wisdom
That's something I could understand

Walk into a Dream

I once knew a working man
Who labored hard for forty years
Married a sturdy woman
Raised three fine kids
And hardly knew their names
He hiked into the woods one day
The next he was never seen
He did not die says I
He walked into his dream

I knew a woman of great beauty
Who lived a life of leisure
She gave her days to comfort
And gave her nights to pleasure
She had a child and married
A man of sufficient means
She breathed her last in a sigh
And walked into her dream

We live a million lives at once
And never know what's real
We learn what's right and wrong
What to think and what to feel
We seek adventures when we can
We work when it's expected
Comes a time we take a stand
And hope that we're respected
In the end we always wonder
Is this what it all means?
We do not die says I
We walk into our dreams

Langston Hughes

Let's not waste our time on petty squabbles
On arguments that never end
America cannot be
What America has never been
Read Langston Hughes
And then you'll see
What America has never been (to me)

Is it all subjective then?
One man's kitchen another's den
We can't go back to a time and place
That does not exist for the human race
It exists for some but not for others
It exists for you but not your brothers

One man's heaven is another's hell
The night Thoreau spent in jail
MLK spent three or four
Malcolm X never found the door
Lakota Apache Cherokee Ho
One man's high is another's low
Cesar Chavez worked for labor
Mexico pleads: Be a good neighbor
Susan Anthony and the suffragettes
Not once have we expressed regret

America is not what it used to be
In most ways it's better
In some it's worse
One man's blessing is another's curse

Lost Arts

Remember when there were letters
Generated by human hands
Not calculated by computers
With voices in foreign lands

Dead and gone
Dead and gone
Gone the way of phonographs
Tasteless jokes and carefree laughs
Gone the way of gingerbread
Have a drink and go to bed

We used to have mass events
Communal homes and cheap rents
We saw new films in cinemas
And understood what people meant

Dead and gone
Dead and gone
Gone the way of rock and roll
Gone the way of soul
Gone the way of privacy
Give a sigh and let it be

We used to let the children play
Visit friends and sometimes stay
Gave them lots of room to roam
Now we keep them safe at home

Dead and gone
Dead and gone

Gone the way of local stores
Gone the way of daily chores
Gone like civil rights
Take a drink and say goodnight

Alone

The company of our fellow beings
The most precious thing on earth
There is nothing of greater value
There is little of equal worth

Music is a delicious gift
As well as poetry and dance
The most fortunate among us
Find a taste of true romance

There is nature in abundance
There is beauty beyond words
There are wonders in this world
Far more than we deserve

There are mountains of granite
Carved out of ancient stone
There are multicolored waterfalls
From nature's golden throne

The many miracles of life
More than we can ever know
Are always so much greater
When we are not alone

Teach Your Children

The way of the world is not determined
It could take most any path
It could go the way of enlightenment
Or choose the way of wrath

Teach your children right and wrong
There is no greater lesson
Help them grow up brave and strong
And always to ask questions

Teach them to respect all others
Without regard to race or creed
We are all equal in human value
Without regard to need

When in doubt do not pretend
Admit that you just don't know
Allow them to discover truth
And give them room to grow

The children will become the teachers
To guide us through the night
If they learn their lessons well
The future will be bright

Machines

Machines machines machines
Machines are everywhere
They're in your living quarters
They chase you up the stairs
They follow you downtown
They greet you at the fair
They take you to the market
And choose your style of hair

Machines machines machines
Machines are everywhere
They get inside your head
They know how much you care
When they disapprove your actions
They look at you and stare
They take you for a ride
They tell you when to share
Machines machines machines
Machines are everywhere

You may live in the mountains
And breathe the mountain air
You may live on an island
In your own private lair
You may live in the desert
So far away no one would dare
But you can't escape their reach
Machines are everywhere

Mind of Mansel

Throw away the rules of grammar
Discard logic and formal structure
Allow imagination free reign
Roll the dice and roll again

Welcome to the mind of Mansel
Where demons rise to heaven
And saints descend to hell
Where the least of all our brethren
Can ring the victory bell

A mechanic from the nether world
Gets lost under the hood
What's good is bad
What's bad is good
The story never ends
Or does what you think it should

He was born to tell a story
And he tells that story well
Welcome to the twists and turns
In the mind of Chris Mansel

Jake's Word

A master of all forms
A man of great vision
He calls forth inspiration
Little need of revision

When tragedy strikes
The halls of humankind
I await the words of wisdom
The compassionate truth
And deepest understanding
That inevitably emerge
From the caverns of his mind

In images pulled
From the highways of time
In free-flowing verse
Or meters of rhyme
He locates the pearls
That speak to the heart
Delivers them through
His timeless art

A man for all seasons
He channels his muse
In chords and rhythms
From folk to blues
His voice holds the secrets
Of so many years
Caring and sharing
The howls of his fears

Of all that I've wondered
And all that I've heard
Few things can rival
The strength of Jake's word

The Wizard of Alabama

I met a man in Nashville
In the company of Mr. Prine
He summoned music from the gods
In harmonies divine

We shared a long hard road
A journey to the west
We played the Zen fantastic
We hope we passed the test

He hailed from Alabama
An oasis in the storm
A man of the enlightenment
Despite where he was born

He took it to the limits
Played it like a carefree gambler
Pushed through the endless night
Like a weary midnight rambler

No one could push it further
No one could risk it all
Like the wizard of Alabama
Who answered fortune's call

Foreboding

You can hear it in the wind
Whispering through the trees
Down the alleys
Through the streets
A gently crying breeze

You can feel it in the blood
Coursing through your veins
In the bones
In the marrow
In the air before it rains

You can see it in the faces
Of the people on the streets
In their smiles
In their laughter
In everyone you meet

You can sense it in the forest
Where the creatures run away
In the hunters
In the hunted
A haunting sense of dismay

You observe it in the sky
An enduring sense of sorrow
Darker blues
Deeper clouds
A striking fear of no tomorrow

Dividing Lines

A word becomes an argument
An argument becomes a feud
A feud becomes who we are
In everything we say and do

It shrouds every picture
And shadows every joy
It marks the heart with sorrow
Like a child with a broken toy

The seed of discontentment
Burrows deep inside
It grows into a bitter pill
That haunts until we die

Division is the story
The scourge of humankind
To overcome our problems
We must erase dividing lines

Dust Bowl

The dust rolled in like a giant wave
Sweeping the land and hills
Swallowing farms like morbid graves
Take cover and write your wills

Oklahomans lined up on the westward trail
To join the farm labor force
To them the American dream had failed
Leaving them without recourse

Mothers with their babes in arm
Fathers desperate to make a buck
Protect their children from all harm
Begging for work and praying for luck

Hard working women and men
Tossed out on a crowded road
Whole families rendered homeless
Like the family of ma and pa Joad

They lived in camps and rode the rails
Derided as ignorant no good bums
When they held a hand out for help
They were spit on and treated like scum

But they held their heads high
And they found a way
Hard times made them stronger
And they're stronger to this day

Katrina

The storm of the century
Did not disappoint
It wiped out New Orleans' lower ninth
Where they were always poor
Now they're desolation row

The real tragedy of Katrina
Is that they were not prepared
They knew it was coming
But they were not prepared
It's as if they didn't care

Now we all live in New Orleans
And the lower ninth is half
The populated world
Venice Miami San Francisco New York
Hong Kong Singapore Tokyo Dubai
All of the port cities
And most of the poor

We know what's coming
And we are not prepared
It's as if we just don't care

Collective Unconscious

That which connects us all
Making the many one
From the most remote tribe in the Amazon
To the high church in Rome
From the oldest temple of Buddha
To the Anastasi cave dwellings
The trinity within the trinity without
The mother the father the great spirit
The father the mother the holy ghost
The past the present the future
The mother the father the child
That which connects each of us
And from the multitudes makes one
In the deepest folds of our unconscious mind
That which binds us to the ancestors
That which links us to our successors
That which hurls us into an unknown
Future with eyes wide shut
The conscious the unconscious the subconscious
The dream the nightmare the waking world
The day the night and twilight
Life death and in between
Our desired needs and possessions
The imagined the perceived the real
The mind the body the heart
The pillars of life faith and art
We are all what we are as all
We are all what we are as one

Woody Guthrie

Woodrow Wilson Guthrie
A man of the people
A man of the hour
A man who stood
Like a granite tower

The man could rhyme
Like breathing the air
Didn't have much money
But what he had he'd share

He grew up in Okemah
In those Oklahoma hills
The ones you still see
In the old picture stills
Life was hard enough but fair
If you had the will
And you took the dare

He lost his sister
In a horrible fire
For a very long time
His mood was dire
But he picked himself up
And he moved ahead
Every morning you make
yourself get out of bed

He knew heartbreak and sweat
From an early age
He learned how to paint

To earn a decent wage

He picked up the guitar
To spread the joy of life
Just a moment of pleasure
To let go of the strife

He lived through hard times
The dust bowl migration
Followed the crops
On the roads of this nation

He sang the songs
That made you understand
How hard life was
For the common man

When they made Woody
They broke the mold
The one they already had
The world could barely hold

Secrets

You entrusted me with secrets
And I will hold them in trust
Yet there are times I wish
I could let them go
Or send them back to you
Like a gift-wrapped package
Unopened and unknown

But while we can delete unwanted
Facts and undesired messages
From our electronic memories
We cannot so easily erase
Such knowledge from our minds

There are secrets that should
Be safely locked away
Where no harm can be done
There are secrets we should bury
And never grant the light of day
To plant them in another's mind
To unsettle and disturb
Is something less than kind

Kindly keep your secrets
Fuel for the fire
Or release them to all the world
Let them breathe the open air
Or choke on their own toxicity
And expire

American Spring

The air implodes with life
Bursts with excitement
Players stand ready
On the field of play
A jump in every step
A smile on every face

Flowers in full bloom
Lovers in the parks
Reclining on lazy blankets
Sipping wine with tender lips
Enchanting glances
A gentle kiss
Tasting the nectar of life

Children laugh dance and play
Carefree cartwheels on the lawn
Butterflies and violins
Ice cream trucks and daffodils
Moms with strollers
Babes with wide eyes
Drinking the sensory feast

Springtime in America
Hope and happiness abound
Somehow we know
It will all be okay
Somehow we sense
It begins again today

Good Morning

(Prayer for a New Beginning)

Good morning in America
Good morning to the world
Today is the day we unify
In the fight against disease
Today is the day we rally
In the battle for equality
Today is the day we break through
In our desire to understand each other
Today is the day we stand up
In the pledge against all war
Today is the day we affirm
A declaration of human rights
Today is the day we push forward
In the quest for universal democracy
Today is the day we resolve ourselves
In the mission to end hunger
Today is the day we move ahead
In the struggle for clean air
Today is the day we commit
In the push to clean the earth
Today is the day we plant the staff
In the effort to save the wilderness
Today is the day we embrace
The knowledge of our unity
In these and all things decent
Good and true

Mitakuye oyasin
We are all one

Greens of Augusta

Like the oranges of Hieronymus Bosch
The greens of Augusta are legendary
Colors explode like symphonies of light
Luminescence dazzles the senses
A separate reality takes hold

Nature announces the onset of life
In displays of color so vivid and bright
It opens the windows of the wanting mind
And stretches the boundaries of dream
In a manner so stunningly bold

The greens of Augusta once seen
Like the staggering blues of Parish
Or the hypnotic shades of Monet
Will never abandon our yearning heart
No matter how often its told

When I've entered my final passage
And I dwell in the halls of what's known
Let me visit once more the greens of Augusta
Let them settle in my resting soul
Then let my story unfold

Obsession

Fixation to the point of madness
Where nothing else exists
There is not another anywhere
There is only this

I have known a life of order
I know exactly what it is
There are so many things of interest
I have made an extensive list

But something grabs ahold of me
It will not let me go
It takes me by the hand
And tells me what I know

For some it's about money
For others it's about a game
For some it's about a lover
In the end it's always the same

Obsession steals a man's soul
Leaves him desperate and lost
For the object of our obsessions
Will exact an unbearable cost

Force Matters Least

Food feeds the body
Wine nourishes the heart
Knowledge fuels the mind
Love nurtures the soul

The people will rise and fight
For food wine and knowledge
But when it comes to conquering armies
Love overcomes them all

Love endures the ages
Love puts all else to shame
Love is love is love
Like a rose by any name

Love climbs the tallest mountain
Love tames the fiercest beast
When everything is on the table
Brute force matters least

The Artist

(for Cal Wenby)

He reveals his secrets
In countless forms
Some stark some subtle
Some harsh some warm

He paints in letters
Overlays of grace
Submerging figures
In mystic lace

To read his mind
You must know his heart
He invests his passion
In the world of art

He is an alchemist
Transforming light
Into visual spectacles
Beyond our sight

He has no fear
Of critical measure
He delivers imagery
That delivers pleasure

He is an artist
Of the highest order
Exceeding boundaries
And crossing borders

Time

Time is a freight train
It bears down on you like rolling thunder
Like a buffalo stampede on the open plains
It beats you down and tramples you
Under waves of pounding hooves
A most horrible refrain

Time is the eye of a raging storm
It comforts you with a sense of calm
Before it yields to nature's wrath
Ripping limb from branch
Uprooting tree from earth
Shattering our chosen path

Time is a river flowing
From a gentle easy rolling stream
To roaring rapids of impending doom
Spawning life to whole ecosystems
Taking death into her sweet embrace
While a deepest darkness looms

Time is a whisper in the darkest forest
Time is the silence of the deepest sea
Time bends folds sits still and rolls
Time is the ultimate mystery

Adversity II

You cannot breach the summit
Without a slip

You cannot cross the river
Without a scare

You cannot complete a journey
Without a detour

You cannot fulfill a life
Without regrets

In any endeavor of importance
In any mission of worth
In any undertaking for any reason
In any venture on this earth
There will be adversity

The greater the objective
The stronger the resistance
Those who embrace adversity
Those who relish the opportunity
Those who take it in stride
Without grief or remorse
Will not only survive but thrive

Adversity is the great teacher
The developer of character

Here is a Man

Here is a man who gave his all
In everything that he did
Here is a man who sacrificed
All he had for his kids
Here is a man who would give
You the shirt he's wearing
Here is a man whose greatest
Asset is the depth of his caring

So when his days alas are done
Let it be said his life was one
Of extraordinary strength and wonder
Days of glory nights of thunder

Let it be said here was a man
Who did not hesitate to take a stand
Who lived according to his creed
Who answered every call of need

Here is a man who was born proud
Who says to the world I am here aloud
Who always had a hand for a brother
Who considered the needs of others

Here is a man who lived
To the highest degree
The life of the man
He wanted to be

National Pride

(for Hideki Matsuyama)

The pride of his nation
He represented with honor and dignity
He faced down the beast of adversity
Not once or twice but thrice
He stared into the abyss
And hunted down the victory
Like a man driven by destiny
He felt enormous pressure
But he would not yield

Few of us will ever feel the kind
Of pressure brought to bear
On this one man's shoulders
The massive weight of generations
The eyes and ears of millions
Their hopes prayers and devotion
All placed in one man's hands

He is a champion for the ages
He will dwell in the house of heroes
All the days of his life
He will dwell in the hall
Of legends forever

How many tears?

How many times must we bear witness?
How many tears must we cry?
How much sorrow must we endure?
How many souls must die?

As we depart the days of winter
And breathe the freshness of spring
It is a time of revival and rebirth
When the robins and angels sing

Yet the time of mourning still lingers
The wail of the nightingale's song
The executioner's gaze still haunts us
With the dead of society's wrong

It seems we will never learn
As it happens again and again
The nightmares of history repeated
The horrors that have always been

So how much blood must flow?
How many tears must we cry
Before we learn beyond knowing
That too many people have died?

(Respect to Bob Dylan)

The Silence of Space

To escape the earth's atmosphere
To emerge in the depths of space
The greatest adventure of our time
Extending the reach of the human race

We have never felt such silence
The absolute absence of sound
There is nothing we can compare
To our experience on earthly ground

Is there something in this silence
That human senses cannot detect?
Something deeply boldly present
Beyond our power to select?

Of all the profound mysteries
Loom the existence of space and time
They capture our imaginations
To expand the human mind

Decline of the Mind

We bear witness over time
A decline in the human mind
No more than we can stand
A small rift in a vast land
A little now a little then
A common fate of elder men
Is it a blessing we cannot perceive?
The storied land we must now leave
For we must journey far away
Into the house of yesterdays
And there to dwell among our peers
Whom life has given yesteryears
Quiet now no longer mourn
For when one passes another's born
And we will all be blessed in time
To find our sorrows turned to rhyme
So in our minds we build a place
Where we will always win the race
Where we are loved and we love others
For all are sisters and all are brothers

The Intelligence of the Body

The body possesses intelligence
It informs the mind of what it needs
Seeking balance grace and nourishment
Healthy patterns is what it breeds

Abuse the mind offend the body
Abuse the body offend the mind
Mind body heart and soul
A balance of the delicate kind

Too often we listen to our hearts
And yield to passions of desire
Too much too soon too often
Can lead to consequence most dire

In following the way of the mind
Far too often we may pretend
We can far exceed our natural limit
Pushing past the point of mend

We often go the way of soul
We have no choice we must
But if the body cannot endure
We can no longer trust

The body is both hearth and home
It must endure our trials and tests
Take care to listen with respect
For the body knows what's best

Hope Rises

Hope rises with a touch of spring
Fruit ripened on the vine
The scent of sun kissed pollen
Clouds of cream and golden glory
A symphony of wine and roses
The sweet and bitter taste of hope

We have bathed ourselves in
Endless waves of sorrow
We have seen the blood red sky
We have marched the mourning dirge
We have witnessed beauty die

Yet we have lived to tell the story
To keep our future's faith alive
So we awaken to this morning
When tears of hope fulfill our eyes
Pray the worst is over now
Pray we have survived

Hope rises with the season
And empties out our shame
We remember all our wonders
Miracles too great to name

Infinite Possibilities

The living universe explodes
with infinite possibilities

Possibilities that exist on every level
of every plain of existence

A black hole contains infinity
within a vacuum of eternal nothingness

A common object be it a lamp
a desk or a pen contains an infinite
amount of subatomic elements
within subatomic elements

We are the sum of all that exists
and all that has ever existed
in this life and all lives before
and after this existence

Every moment contains eternity
Every sunset is forever
There are no ends only beginnings
The world overflows with possibilities
Infinite possibilities

We possess the power
to select our experience
to choose the moments that form
the building blocks of our lives

Everything that was is

Everything that is will always be
In that there is hope and prayer
In that there is eternal being

Dignity

I am a proud man
In this I am everyone
I have crossed the seven seas
I have climbed the fiercest mountain
I have faced the beast and lived
I have witnessed the wonders of the universe
Explored the farthest reaches of space
Captured the mysteries of the heart
Lost my way in a maze of dreams
and known what awestruck means

I have created works of beauty
Drawn tears from the eyes of men
I have known the truth of love
I have felt the sting of betrayal
I have celebrated many victories
and learned the lessons of defeat

When you have taken all else
My sight my soul my memories
Be merciful have sympathy
Leave me with my dignity

Without dignity what reason is there
to remain in this world of wonder?

Untamed

There are those who inform the heavens
There are those who command the seas
There are those who inspire tributes
and those who cure disease

Yet there are few who can match his passion
Fewer still who can reach the hearts
of ordinary men and women
Who can move them to play their parts

For he speaks the language of the people
The masses who have no names
Who expect poetry to rhyme or sing
Not to play poetic games

He will not win the poets prize
He is omitted from their praise
Yet his voice will find a place
When the people must be raised

ABOUT THE AUTHOR

Jack Random has devoted most of his life to writing. His roots firmly planted in the fertile central valley of California, he has marched the streets in protest, haunted jazz town bars, read poetry in cafes and town squares, strutted his hour upon the stage, crisscrossed the country by air, rail, highway and thumb, mourned at Wounded Knee, gazed into the eyes of the crow at Grand Canyon, and paid tribute at the grave of Geronimo. He has labored in the fields of plenty, toiled on the assembly line, pursued higher education, and attempted to inspire children in the public schools. He has been a pilgrim and a seeker of truth. He is married to the love of his life.

OTHER WORKS BY JACK RANDOM

Jack Random has published eight novels:

Ghost Dance Insurrection (A Jazzman Novel) *
Wasichu: The Killing Spirit
Number Nine: The Adventures of Jake Jones and Ruby
Daulton
A Patriot Dirge (A Jazzman Novel)
Hard Times: The Wrath of an Angry God
Pawns to Players: The Stairway Scandal
Pawns to Players: A Match for the White House
Pawns to Players: The Putin Gambit

Two volumes of plays:

Random Plays, Vol. I: D'Arc Underground and Other Plays
Random Plays, Vol. II: Aphrodite House and Other Plays

Three collections of short stories:

Apache Jack: Native Visions and Stories
Random Jack: Tales from Jazztown
Random Jack Children's Hour: Stories for Young Minds

And a collection (ten volumes) of political essays:

Jazzman Chronicles, Volumes I-X

* Ghost Dance Insurrection was originally published by Dry
Bones Press. All works published by Crow Dog Press.

www.ingramcontent.com/pod-product-compliance
Lightning Source LLC
Chambersburg PA
CBHW051057030726
47504CB00006B/1676